Willow Run

Willow Run

PATRICIA REILLY GIFF

WENDY
LAMB
BOOKS

J Giff

Published by
Wendy Lamb Books
an imprint of
Random House Children's Books
a division of Random House, Inc.
New York

Wendy Lamb Books is a trademark of Random House, Inc.

Visit us on the Web! www.randomhouse.com/kids
Educators and librarians, for a variety of teaching tools, visit us at
www.randomhouse.com/teachers

Library of Congress Cataloging-in-Publication Data is available upon request.

ISBN: 0-385-73067-5 (trade)
        0-385-90096-1 (lib. bdg.)

The text of this book is set in 12-point Goudy.

Book design by Kenny Holcomb

Printed in the United States of America

September 2005

10 9 8 7 6 5 4 3 2 1

BVG

FOR MY GRANDSON,

WILLIAM LANGAN GIFF,

WITH LOVE

Chapter One

The wheels made a horrible sound; no wonder. The wagon belonged to Joey Kind down the block, who hadn't used it in years; the whole thing was a rusted mess. And the nerve of Joey to say, "You be careful, Meggie Dillon. Don't ruin it."

Too bad, I wanted to tell him, *keep your old wagon.* But I had to borrow it. It was all for the war effort. And right now rattling along in the center of the wagon was Big Bertha, Mom's iron statue that had a clock in her stomach. She'd been rusting away in the attic forever, just like Joey's wagon.

Big Bertha was going to war. Mr. North at the junkyard would pay me a quarter and Bertha would be melted down into bullets. Poor Bertha.

It was almost dark so I began to hurry. I chugged past Grandpa's house but I knew he wasn't there. He was at my house waiting for Dad to get home from work. Dad had news, that was all Mom would tell us, and we'd hear it over a late supper of salad greens and flounder in tomato sauce: greens we'd grown in Grandpa's garden, and flounder Grandpa and I had caught this morning. Poor flounder. Poor me for having to eat it with every single one of its skinny bones getting caught in my teeth.

Someone was moving along the side of Grandpa's house. My mouth went dry. Here we were in the middle of a war. Suppose it was a spy?

As quietly as I could considering the squeak of the wheels, I shoved the wagon into a pile of bushes and tiptoed up the driveway. I went slowly, ready to tear back to the street and across the lawn to one of Grandpa's neighbors before the spy shot me.

A pair of shadows. I clapped my hand to my mouth so I wouldn't make a sound. Then I realized I knew them both. One was Joey Kind's older brother, Mikey, and the other was a kid I had seen down at the beach flexing his muscles as if he were Charles Atlas, the weight lifter. His name was Tommy or Donny or . . . I wasn't sure, but I remembered my friend Lily Mollahan nudging me, asking, "Did you ever see such an idiot in your life?"

He was not only an idiot, he was big. They were

both big, sixteen or seventeen, and tough, and I shivered thinking what would happen if they caught me following them.

But what were they doing? They had an open can of red paint and a couple of brushes, and they began to dab something on Grandpa's kitchen window.

"Hey!" I yelled, without stopping to think.

They spun around. Mikey looked embarrassed, but the muscle guy kept going with the brush. It looked as if he were painting a spider . . . but then I saw. He was painting a swastika, the Nazi sign, on the glass pane.

"That's what we do to Nazis around here," he said.

"He's not a Nazi!" I could feel the anger in my chest, a pain so sharp it was almost hard to breathe. "He's American," I managed.

"Sounds German to me." The muscle guy was grinning. And then he was imitating Grandpa, mixing up his *f*s and his *v*s, sounding the way the Nazis did in the movies . . .

. . . sounding like Grandpa.

I had a quick picture of Grandpa in my mind, Grandpa sitting on a bench down at the canal, his head back, that awful red hat on his head, his face sunburned, singing "Mairzy Doats" with a German accent.

"Get out of here, both of you!" I yelled, almost forgetting it would be dark in about two minutes and I was alone with them back there.

"You're lucky," Muscle Man said. "If this were anywhere else but Rockaway, they'd probably put him in jail. He's got to be a spy."

I picked up a stone, ready to throw it, but Mikey took a step toward me. "You know what, Meggie? I think you want the Nazis to win the war. You and your Nazi grandfather."

My arm went down to my side. "That's not true. You know that's—"

"Anywhere else, something would happen to him. Worse than jail," Mikey said. "Worse than anything. And to you, too."

Why was he saying this? Maybe because I'd told the lifeguard at the beach that he was out too far.

But maybe not. He'd always been mean.

Or maybe that was what people really thought, that Grandpa was a spy, that I . . .

Somewhere down the block I heard a door slam. The two of them slipped past me along the side of the house. When they were halfway down the driveway I plunked the stone after them, hitting the pail of paint.

"Crummy aim," Muscle Man said, and Mikey called, "*Heil* Hitler."

"Watch out, next time—" and then I broke off because it looked as if they were going to come back after me.

I darted around back, but now I heard them marching up the street yelling, "*Heil, heil,*" with that same accent.

I went up to Grandpa's window and put my finger on the painted swastika. It was thick and still shiny wet, and I could feel that my cheeks were wet, too.

Grandpa was the biggest pest in the whole world, calling me Margaret every two minutes instead of Meggie, whispering during movies so I couldn't even hear what was going on, saying *bah* whenever he didn't agree with me.

So why was I crying?

Grandpa who loved Rockaway, who told me that Hitler was a maniac. Grandpa who had cried when he told me about hiking in the Hartz Mountains when he was a boy, who cried, too, when he talked about the terrible things that were happening in Germany. What would he say if he saw that swastika?

I went around back to his garage. I was glad I knew where every single thing was. Right away I put my hand on the can of turpentine, found an old rag, and stood there crying as I wiped the paint off the window.

It took a long time, but that was all right. I couldn't go home and let everyone see that my eyes were red. If Mom thought something was wrong she'd start to question me . . . and wouldn't let go until I was cornered.

After I finished, I put the turpentine can back in the garage. I wiped my hands with the rag, then stuck it down deep in Grandpa's garbage can.

Big Bertha and the wagon could stay in the bushes

tonight. She'd have to go to war tomorrow, and Joey Kind's wagon could park there forever without getting any worse than it was now.

I wiped my eyes with the back of my hand. Then I started home to hear Dad's news.

Chapter Two

Mom was at the door. "The fish is like a piece of cardboard, the salad wilted, everyone wondering where you were."

"Sorry." I reached up to give her a quick kiss.

She kissed back, then wrinkled her nose. "What's that smell?"

Grandpa came out of the dining room. "Margaret and I never catch cardboard fish."

I wanted to tell him for about the hundredth time not to call me Margaret, but at least he had distracted Mom.

"Let's eat," she said. "Dad has been waiting to tell us . . ."

And there was Dad at the table, grinning, his eyes big behind his glasses. It made me think of the bird game my brother, Eddie, and I always played. Dad was an owl in those glasses with the heavy frames, and Mom a plump pigeon like the ones who flew around Sonny Breitenback's coop, always busy fixing up their nests with bits of straw and pieces of ribbon.

Eddie and I could never figure out what Grandpa was. "Something big, wings flapping all over the place," I always said. Eddie agreed; then he said I was a Canadian goose, always stretching my neck into everyone's business.

Eddie was definitely one of those red-winged blackbirds who appeared every March, looking plain until they fluttered their wings; *Talk to me, talk to me,* they always said. The redwings were my favorites, hands down, and so was Eddie, with his round face and the gap between his square front teeth.

Grandpa gave me a nudge. "So where are you, Margaret?" *Vhere.*

"Right here."

"Well?" *Vell.*

They were staring at my sleeve. I took a look; it was a smear of red paint I hadn't noticed in the dark. Suppose I hadn't gotten all the paint off the window?

Grandpa would never say anything, but I knew he would wonder about it. He might mutter *bah* to himself, but how would he feel?

"Where did you get that lipstick?" Mom ran a spatula under the fish, which was curling up around the edges.

"Looks like Victory Red." I pulled out my sleeve to see it

better: it was just like the lipstick Lily Mollahan smeared on her mouth as soon as her grandmother was out of sight.

"Listen." Dad pushed at his glasses. We stopped talking as he held out his hands. "My news." He took a breath. "There's a top-security factory that makes bombers, B-24s. Great planes that are going to win the war for us."

Dad loved planes. Before he found out he had trouble seeing and needed those Coke-bottle glasses, he'd been a barnstormer, flying planes all over the country, going to every air show he could find.

I took a bite of the fish; it was the worst thing I had ever tasted.

"So what's the news?" Grandpa said, chewing, picking bones out of his mouth at the same time.

"I have a chance to be a foreman at the factory," Dad said, beaming at us. "Can you imagine doing something so important for the war effort!"

I could feel my mouth opening.

"It takes four days to get there," Dad said, "a place called Willow Run, Michigan."

We put down our forks. Who could eat that poor dried-up fish, anyway? I swallowed and Muscle Man was back in my head, that mean look on his face. What had he said? Something like *"Your grandfather would be arrested anywhere else."*

And what had Dad said? *"Top-security"? "Important for the war effort"?* In my mind was a picture of a movie

Grandpa and I had seen. It was about G-men and the OSS and German spies all over the place. Wouldn't they be at the factory looking for spies, too?

Oh, Grandpa.

"Will we all go?" I said in a small voice.

Dad sighed. "The only thing is," he said, "I heard the apartment isn't great. Two postage-stamp bedrooms, a pull-out couch in the living room."

A way out. "So not Grandpa," I said quickly, my throat burning. "Too small."

Grandpa turned to look at me.

I could see tears in Mom's eyes. She put her hand on Grandpa's arm. "How could we ask you to take such a trip? To give up your house and your garden?"

One thing I knew—Grandpa couldn't come with us. Before Grandpa could answer, I cut in. "Suppose Eddie comes home on leave? Suppose he just comes home and none of us are here?"

My heart was pounding. Grandpa had to stay here. Had to. And then I thought about his being here alone. Mom must have been thinking the same thing. She took a quick breath. And at the same time Grandpa said, "Ah, Edward." *Edvard.*

I swallowed. Eddie was his favorite.

"You're right, all of you. I will stay here," Grandpa said.

I looked out the window. I had a sudden memory of sloshing through the rain with Grandpa, laughing.

We sat there, all of us silent. Then Mom jumped up to bring out dessert: canned peaches, slimy as eels, and Social Tea crackers. And after a while Grandpa put down his napkin. "Maybe we'll fish again tomorrow, Margaret."

Mom shredded out the fish bones and put what was left on waxed paper for Judy and Jiggs, the cats. They didn't think it was cardboard; they were thrilled.

I went upstairs to take my bath, scraping another smear of red off my ankle. What would Willow Run be like without Grandpa around every two minutes?

I stopped scrubbing. At least he'd never be arrested here with his neighbors, Mrs. Easterly on one side, Mr. Noonan on the other. I picked up the soap again. Willow Run. I told myself I was going to have an adventure, the greatest adventure of my life. So why did I feel so bad?

Chapter Three

A few days later, I tiptoed around upstairs. If Mom heard me, she'd have me down in the kitchen in two seconds: *Just spear those pickles into the glass dish, Meggie,* or *Spread a little cream cheese on those chunks of celery, please.*

I leaned way out the bedroom window now, looking for Grandpa: my head, neck, both arms, and belt buckle scraping the sill, my shoe tips scraping the floor.

The shoes were all scratched up from the beach. Mom would have a fit when she saw them. "Leather is rationed, Meggie. *Rationed,*" she'd said, almost crying, when I had left my Sunday ones in the rain last month.

I inched out farther. In back of the houses the Atlantic

Ocean crashed itself up on the sand, and seagulls screeched as they fought over dinner. In front was the gravel road. And any minute Grandpa would march down that road, bringing a salad for our going-to-Willow-Run-to-win-the-war party.

Grandpa hadn't found out about the red paint swastika. "I'll bring the best salad you've ever tasted," he had promised this morning. Grandpa was in love with food. He and I grew most of it in his jungle of a garden out behind his house. Then we'd trundle it all into his kitchen to snip, and chop, and dice. . . .

"Slice finely, if you don't mind, Margaret, we don't need onion slices the size of elephant feet."

I scrambled all the way out the window and across the roof to get a better look at the road. Grandpa would be on time, I knew that; he always was. Four o'clock on the dot.

The church bells began to bong, and there he was.

Bingo.

But good grief. His red plaid hat was clamped down on his head on a day you could fry an egg on the sidewalk! In his outstretched hands, wrapped in see-through waxed paper, was an *Apfelstrudel*.

What happened to the salad?

Strudel! I would never have thought of it before. But now I realized. A German dessert right in the middle of the war with Germany. What would people think!

I yanked myself back in through the window, stepped

over my suitcase, packed and ready to go, and went downstairs to the party, the neighbors jammed into the living room and spilling out onto the porch.

The back door opened; Grandpa filled up the whole space. "Ah, Mar-gar-et." He held out the strudel.

"An apple pie." I grabbed it before he could correct me. "What happened to the salad, for Pete's sake?" I whispered, and then, "Meggie. Don't call me Margaret."

I didn't wait to hear what I knew he'd say next: "It's your grandmother's name, nothing wrong with Margaret."

Too old, too grown-up, I said in my head. I put the strudel on the dining room table, maneuvering a crumb off the edge and onto my tongue. It was my favorite, after all.

I slid away from the table, the taste filling my mouth, as Mom came in with more plates. She spotted my shoes and raised her eyes toward the ceiling.

The front doorbell rang three times, *bing bing bing.* It was my best friend, Lily. She loved the sound of our chimes. She didn't wait for someone to answer but marched right in, her grandmother shaking her head in back of her, as Mom went to say hello.

Lily came into the dining room and looked under a covered dish. "Spam, I knew it."

"Well, young ladies." Mr. Colgan came toward us before we could escape, a fistful of peanuts disappearing into his mouth. "Ah, Meggie. Going halfway across the country with your mom and dad, are you?"

I nodded.

Lily bent over to pet the cats under the table. I didn't blame her. Who wanted to be captured by Mr. Colgan?

"I was in Michigan once," he began. "Did I ever tell you about that? It was in the thirties . . ."

He might keep me there forever. I circled around him, pretending to straighten the picture on the side table: my brother, Eddie, in his uniform, grinning, a space between his front teeth.

Virginia Tooey, Eddie's girlfriend, came over to look at the picture, too. She smiled at me, and I smiled back. She was the prettiest girl I'd ever seen, with her curly hair and Chiclet teeth. Eddie thought so, too.

In back of me, Mr. Colgan was saying, "Four days to get to Michigan. You'll be a long way from your grandfather."

An odd thing about Eddie's picture. When I moved it around, it seemed his smiling eyes always followed me. Just beyond the table was the window to the ocean, a sunbeam cutting a path through the water. Suppose I could slide across it all the way to Europe? Would Eddie be there, arms out, waiting to dance me around? Or maybe he was still at Fort Dix in New Jersey, safe, no one shooting at him. Then he'd come home on leave to sit on the bench with Grandpa in his garden or jitterbug with Virginia Tooey at the dance hall on 102nd Street.

We hadn't had a letter from Eddie in seventeen days. Every morning Mom pretended to dust the table, her cloth circling the lamp as she watched the road for the mailman.

She had asked the mailman over and over to remember that we'd have a new address soon, so worried that Eddie's letters might not get to us.

Please, Eddie, let there be a letter tomorrow. Tell us you weren't at the D-day landing in Normandy. That's what Mom and Dad need to hear.

I told myself I wasn't worried, not one bit. The last thing Eddie had said to me was *"It will be a big adventure, Meggie, that's what this'll be. And just think, you'll be the only one home, the princess. No more baby."*

"Ha. You think I'll get double desserts, double allowance, and Grandpa won't be telling me how wonderful you are every two minutes?"

I went over to the table, happy to see that Mr. Colgan was telling Lily's grandmother about the price of bread and cake and canned beans. I helped myself to supper: a little Spam doctored up with Grandpa's pickles, a mountain of Mom's potato salad with a couple of elephant-foot onion slices, and a lump of oleo for the heel of the rye bread. I went outside to sit with Lily on the back step.

"The oleo is disgusting, isn't it?" I looked down at the white lump with yellow dye running through it in spots, wartime butter.

"Horrible," Lily agreed.

"I wouldn't smear it on my bread in a million years except that I'm entering an oleo contest, twenty-five words or less."

"Great," Lily mumbled, her mouth full.

"*Mmm, mmm, mmm, the tastiest taste in the world, oleo even . . .* ," I began, and broke off. "That's as far as I've gotten."

Lily sat there nodding and I thought about Grandpa. He was going to skip the oleo contest. "I can't think of one good thing about it," he had told me.

I looked back through the doorway. He was talking about our soldiers landing in Normandy now, shaking his head over the casualties. His voice was loud . . . and you could hear the German in it, the roll of the *rrrr*s, the mixed-up *f*s and *v*s. "We have to hope," he said. *Haf to hope.*

I wondered what Lily thought about his accent. But she was speaking at the same time. "I'm going to miss you."

I couldn't help feeling sorry for her. I was going to have this tremendous adventure, and she was stuck in Rockaway.

Lily turned to me. "About the candy," she began.

I swallowed. Lily and I had found a bag of candy that Mom had planned on sending to Eddie. We had eaten a ton of it.

"I'm sorry about that," she said.

My mouth watered when I thought of it. "Just as well we ate some of it," I said, feeling a little guilty anyway. "Eddie always gets cavities."

"But your mom," Lily said.

I didn't answer. Mom had been furious about sending only half the candy. We went back inside then, and I edged around to Grandpa, who was still wearing that miserable hat, and tapped his arm. "I'll take that for you."

His hand went up absently, his thin hair rising as he slid the hat off his head.

With my plate in one hand I went to the kitchen door and tossed the hat onto a chair. Dad was cutting into a huge watermelon at the counter. He grinned when he saw the hat. And Virginia Tooey had come into the kitchen. Mom, an apron tied around her middle, was leaning against the sink talking to her, smiling. Mom was round as a dumpling, but when she smiled there was no one as pretty.

She handed me a plate of celery and olives. "Meggie, just put this . . ." She turned back to Virginia without finishing.

I found a place for it on the dining room table and stood next to Lily. Jiggs meowed underneath and I bent over to give him a taste of Spam. He took one sniff, then walked away. "I don't blame him," I told Lily.

And there was Mr. Colgan, everyone veering away from him as if he were the blind man in blindman's buff. "Bet you'll miss your grandpa." He leaned forward to spear a slice of cheese and fly it over my shoulder into his mouth.

I knew Grandpa could hear him. "Dad has a job for the war effort," I said. "We'll be home as soon as it's over."

Mr. Colgan reached for another slice of cheese, his eyes glued to me so I couldn't escape. "Hey, Meggie. Why isn't your grandfather going with you? Plenty of room in the car." He nudged me. "Isn't that a great idea?"

I wished I could back away from him and slide out the door. Grandpa's eyes were on me now. I didn't want to look at him, but my eyes went up to his face. Was he sad that we were going without him?

I could feel it in my chest: no one knew me in Michigan. No one knew that Grandpa had taught me to count in German: *eins, zwei, drei, vier, fünf*; no one like Mikey or the Muscle Man would wonder if Grandpa and I were secretly hoping that Germany would win the war. No one would lock him up in a prison there . . . or worse.

"How can I leave?" Grandpa said. "I have a garden to grow, and I have to wait for Eddie. . . ."

I took another forkful of potato salad. "Right," I said to Mr. Colgan. "He has to stay here."

He'd be safer in Rockaway, even those boys had said so.

And then it was time for Lily and her grandmother to leave. I went to the door with them, still thinking about Grandpa, and gave Lily a hug.

"See you soon," she said.

"After the war." I wondered how long that would be.

"Just for the duration." We both smiled. That was what everyone said all the time.

Chapter Four

Last day. I said goodbye to Lily one last time and sneaked her a key to our house so she could go up to the attic and write a book. I'd even left a piece of candy for her up there.

I skated down the street trying to miss the cracks as I counted blue stars in the windows: six of them, six families who had soldiers fighting in the war, and one gold star in the Winstons' window for Eddie's friend Bobby, a great basketball player, who had been killed in action.

We had a blue star in our own window for Eddie. For a quick moment I closed my eyes thinking about him, his forehead always sunburned, his cap pushed back over his hair.

A letter had finally arrived this morning. It crinkled in

my pocket. I reached in to touch it, Eddie's writing all over it, then turned up Grandpa's path. The banner with his star for Eddie was looped over the knocker on the door instead of hanging in the window like everyone else's. That was Grandpa. Always different.

"Hey, Grandpa?" I unstrapped my skates and left them on the stoop, then took a few giant steps through the living room and into the kitchen. A row of jars marched along the counter, pickle jars, but not holding pickles. Each one had a half-dead sprig of a plant that Grandpa was bringing back to life. Here and there ghostly roots were beginning to sprout.

"Grandpa?" I called again.

Not in the house. Of course not. Outside in his victory garden with the bugs and spiny cucumbers. Ah, not cucumbers yet, just yellow buds. It was only the beginning of July, after all.

I banged out of the kitchen into the yard, catching my heel. I had a hundred blisters from that screen door. But no more. After today I wouldn't see that door again, nor Grandpa's counter filled with jars of green things, nor the cucumber vat on the linoleum floor with pickles swimming around inside. Not until the end of the war. I swallowed thinking of it.

"He's probably out there in the yard dreaming about pickle relish," I said to myself, but under my breath. Lots of things were wrong with Grandpa, but being deaf wasn't one. He always heard more than I wanted him to.

Right. There he was, but he wasn't bent over like a pretzel pulling weeds out of his victory garden. He was under the only tree in the whole yard, a pile of papers on his lap, his red plaid cap pulled down over his eyes.

Why was he just sitting there?

I felt a clutch somewhere in my chest. Grandpa was old. He had even been in the U.S. Army in the Great War. He still talked about it even though it must have been a million years ago, when he had first come to this country from Germany.

Suppose he was dead?

He reached up to wave away a Japanese beetle. They were all over the place, chomping away at the vegetables as fast as he planted them.

I walked toward him. He was alive, certainly he was alive. What was I thinking of? He had told me once he wanted to live to be a hundred. And he still had a way to go.

He looked up from under his bushy eyebrows and pushed back his hat with one large hand. A rim of dirt lined his nails: he was always running a clump of soil between his fingers or sifting it across his wrist, then rubbing it in.

"When your grandmother Margaret died," he had told me once, "I felt better kneeling in the dirt, watching my plants grow. That and . . ." His voice trailed off. Grandpa could drive you crazy, beginning a sentence and stopping halfway through.

"What?" I had asked.

"Edward," he had said. *Edvard.* "And you." He pointed at me. "You make me feel better. Who knows why?"

"Bah," I had answered, his favorite word, pleased in spite of myself. We had grinned at each other.

"Well, Margaret," he said now. *Vell, Mar-gar-et.*

"Meggie."

Grandpa hauled himself to his feet, papers scattering. One landed at my toes: our entry for the Sweetheart Soap contest. I scooped it up. "There's mud all over this. We spent two hours working on it and now . . ."

He peered down at the splotched paper in my hand. "It's not how it looks, Margaret. It's the words we have here." *Verds.* He tapped the paper with his thumb. "We might even win this time."

Impossible. No one would want to touch this. "Think, Grandpa. It's a *soap* contest."

He threw back his head and laughed. His laugh was the best thing about him. Eddie and I always said so. His teeth were strong and even below his gray mustache, and his eyes crinkled, almost like the pictures of Santa Claus in Macy's window every Christmas. When Grandpa laughed, we couldn't help laughing, too.

"I sent an entry to the oatmeal contest," I told him. "I'm probably going to win that, anyway."

I wouldn't win in a hundred years.

"Nasty stuff, that oatmeal," he said.

I nodded. Suppose I did win? I'd have to eat oatmeal for breakfast the rest of my life. That was the prize. A lifetime supply of oatmeal.

I wondered what the prize for the oleo contest was. But winning was winning. Grandpa and I had a plan. When we won our first contest we were going to take ourselves on the bus to New York City and see the sights. It was a secret, of course. Only Eddie knew.

Grandpa looked at his watch. "Enough time to weed a little?"

I let the paper drop back into the pile. "I just came to say goodbye. Mom and Dad said they'd be over later."

"I counted," he said. "Fourteen blossoms on the first cucumber vine."

I didn't like the way his eyes looked, almost the way they did when he dusted the picture of my grandmother Margaret in his living room . . . the only thing he dusted in the whole house.

If I said "Come with us," would he leave his house and his garden? I thought he might. But what about the swastika on his window, and the factory, and the OSS? I thought of prison. I couldn't ask him.

"You'll have fourteen cucumbers." I tried not to look at him.

He walked past me down the path, patting the flat leaves as if they were his babies.

I remembered suddenly. "I have a letter in my pocket. Mom said to bring it over for you to read."

He still didn't answer.

Was Grandpa crying?

Of course not.

I handed him the letter, the thin envelope with red, white, and blue edges. He stood there, patting it the way he had patted the plants, then leaned against the tree to read it.

It wasn't much to read, I knew that, and it had been written two months ago: still April, when the plants hadn't even begun to sprout in Grandpa's garden. Much too soon to know if Eddie had been in Normandy. I knew the letter by heart.

. . . *the war has to end one of these days. In the meantime I think of you and miss you, Mom and Dad, Meggie, Grandpa, and even the cats. I'll be home when this is over, and I can't wait.*

Grandpa crumpled the envelope, and now I was sure he *was* crying. "I'm glad Mrs. Easterly is next door," I said to fill up the no-talking space.

Grandpa turned, his eyes rimmed with red. "Don't you worry about me, Margaret."

"I'm not worried, not one bit."

"Good thing."

I didn't even want to mention the garden. "Maybe you could go fishing with . . ." I couldn't think of anyone.

"I'll go by myself. Probably catch my dinner every day

without anyone knocking over the bait box and splashing her feet in the water."

I bit the inside of my lip. Fishing with Grandpa was just the opposite of what he was saying. He was the one who couldn't move two inches without dropping the hooks into the water, never to be seen again.

Last week the ham sandwiches had gone off the bridge. A bunch of killies had attacked the bread like piranhas, and the brown paper bag with the napkins had sunk to the bottom, one soggy mess. All we had between us was six cents. We didn't have anything to eat all day but a pair of Chiclets he found in his pocket.

"Pay attention," he said now.

"I am."

"What did I say?"

I tried to think. What was he always saying? "You're going to fertilize . . ."

"No."

"You're going to . . . ah . . . go to the movies without me." I took a wild guess. "*Stage Door Canteen.*"

"That hasn't been there for months." He handed me Eddie's crumpled letter. "Don't lose this, now."

"I'm not the one . . . ," I began, and gave up.

"Come on," he said, "I'll show you something inside."

I followed him into the small room in back of the kitchen, his office. The desk took up most of the room and was filled with contest entries, and bills, and newspaper clippings. A small table was covered with pictures: Mom when she was a girl, Eddie and me, one of Grandma Margaret standing in front of the Neckar River in Heidelberg, where she had grown up. But the best thing, Grandpa always said, was his Victory medal from the Great War. I picked it up. The rainbow ribbon was faded and the medal was tarnished, but Grandpa kept it in the place of honor next to Margaret's picture.

"You must have been brave to get this," I said.

Grandpa leaned over my shoulder and touched the angel on the front. "It's the other way around. It reminds me to be brave when I need to be." He stared out the window. "You have to dig deep before you judge a person," he said absently. "What do people say? You can't tell a book by its cover."

What was that all about? I wondered. Had he somehow found out about the swastika on his window? Or maybe he was embarrassed about his accent. It was the first time I'd ever thought of that. Could he possibly know I didn't want him to come to Willow Run?

I glanced over at his second-best thing: a paper tacked up between the windows that said he was a citizen: Josef von Frisch, a new American. The paper was so old it was crinkled on the corners, and it had a damp spot from the hurricane when I was five. It also had a dab of jelly, Eddie's fingerprint from long ago. If I had done that, Grandpa wouldn't have spoken to me for days. As it was, he had just rubbed at it, making it worse.

Grandpa opened one of the drawers; it was stuffed to the gills, as he would say, with all kinds of junk. He pulled out an envelope and rubbed it against his vest before he handed it to me.

I looked down at his loop-de-loop writing: *lettuce, cukes, and tomatoes*; then shook the envelope.

I glanced up at him. "What's this for . . . seeds all mixed together?"

"What do you think? Salad, that's what it is. Plant it all when you get to Michigan."

"All right."

"Bah. You'll probably lose it."

I tried to think of an answer, but he was on his way outside again, banging the screen door behind him.

Willow Run, Michigan
Thursday, I think
    Dear Grandpa,

        We couldn't find anyplace to stay last night, so we slept in the car. I counted nine mosquito bites on one leg and four on the other.

        The cats hate this trip. Judy keeps attacking the floor pads. Jiggs keeps attacking my feet.

        People in a Model A Ford just like ours were

parked next to us. They were on their way to work in a war factory, too, but in the opposite direction.

A girl was crying next to the window. But not me.

Meggie

Chapter Five

The car was filthy, caked with mud from a thunderstorm in Rochester, grit from a blast of wind in Ohio, and a smear of greasy yellow dirt on the fender from somewhere in Michigan.

"We're here," Dad said.

Here was nowhere. A long building that went on forever, cars pulling up in front, people streaming in and out the doors like Macy's. What had I expected Willow Run to be like? I tried to think. Maybe the Emerald City in *The Wizard of Oz*. At least someplace shiny and beautiful.

"It's the factory." Dad waved his hand. "Henry Ford's assembly line for the war effort."

I didn't know who Henry Ford was, didn't know what an assembly line was, and I didn't care. I was sticking to the backseat of the car, boiling hot, while the two cats were fur coats covering my feet. "We're going to live in a factory?"

"Come on, get out. I'll show you," he said.

We walked through the gates. Dad showed a tag to a woman at a table; then we poked our heads into the wide doorway. It was hot, it was noisy, people were all over the place, and pieces of metal were on tables and . . .

"Enough for now," Dad said. "Mom is hot in the car."

We slid back in and Dad waved his arm toward the factory. "Instead of cars, Ford is making bombers, B-24s. The same way though—everyone working on one piece at a time." His round glasses glinted in the sunlight. "It's a mile long, this factory, the largest in the world. If only I could fly one of those B-24s . . ." He broke off. "But the next best thing is to build them."

Mom turned toward him, her plump hand on his arm, her face red from the heat. "I know how much you miss flying."

For a moment no one said anything. We watched people going in and out, hundreds of them, it seemed. If Dad had been able to fly, he'd have been in the war like Eddie. I was glad he wasn't, glad he wore those owl glasses. "I might die of thirst in this car," I said to make him laugh.

He did laugh. "Just the last few streets to go." He started

the car and drove along blocks of apartment houses with a few trailers here and there and a couple of shacks leaning against each other. Not a garden in sight.

Grandpa would hate it.

"All this was thrown up in about two minutes to house the workers," Dad said. "It must have been beautiful before the war, green fields and trees, and once maybe a stream."

"It'll be lovely again," Mom said. "Someday soon."

I knew she was thinking about Eddie coming home, wishing it were soon.

Dad turned the corner and I could see an ice cream truck hugging the curb, SUNDAE, MONDAY, AND ALWAYS painted on the side. A boy about Eddie's age was leaning against the side, jingling the bells.

Dad stopped the car. "Three sundaes, please." He held out a bunch of change. "Strawberry, I guess."

I looked up over the paper I was working on, a contest for Renkens milk, and waved at the boy with my pencil, but he didn't smile. His hair fell over his face, almost hiding his eyes. He stuck his head inside the square opening of his truck and backed out to hand us our ice creams with wooden spoons on top.

What a grouch.

And he'd given us chocolate.

As we drove away I looked back. I pulled my braid over my upper lip to make a tan Hitler mustache and raised my arm in a Nazi salute. "*Heil* Hitler," I yelled.

My friend Lily loved that face.

"What?" Mom said.

"Nothing," I said back, watching as the ice cream boy began to laugh. His whole face changed; then he walked around the side of the truck where I couldn't see him.

I turned around to watch the street as I licked the ice cream off the lid. Every single apartment was the same. Gray. Not a curtain on a window.

"People come and go," Dad said. "Some of them come for the war effort, and some to make money for the first time in their lives. Such good jobs."

He turned the key and the hum of the motor stopped. It was strange to hear the silence. "Anyway," he said. "We're here for the duration." He opened the door and wandered up the walk.

A kindergarten kid could have drawn it: a long low box that stretched from one end of the paper to the other, no paint, no color. And if you divided the box into tiny sections, each family would have one to live in. Worst of all, there was no grass, nothing growing, only tree stumps near the curb, their tops pale and raw. I remembered what Grandpa had said once, shaking his head in anger. "To kill a tree!"

I could see that Mom was as disappointed as I was. I handed the cats to her, one by one, then backed out of the car.

Dad was already turning the key in the lock. Mom

looked over her shoulder at me, her roly-poly face flushed. "It's just for the duration."

The duration again. Hadn't I heard that a hundred times! As if the war were going to end tomorrow.

Mom went up the path with Judy, the mother cat, digging her front claws into her shoulder. The cats thought it was crazy we were here instead of home.

I was beginning to think so, too, but I wasn't going to let anyone know that, especially the kids who were standing at the edge of the walk staring at us. And not only that, people were wandering around all over the place: two women circling around me swinging lunch pails; a girl slapping a jump rope on the cement—*"Strawberry shortcake cream on top, tell me the name of your sweetheart"*—a man at a window, his radio blaring war news.

Someone was playing a song on a Victrola; it was scratchy and skipped a little: *"We'll meet again, don't know where, don't know when."* I'd heard that song over and over. I went around the side of the car, trying not to think about our house on the canal. Instead, I traced my name on the hood with one finger: *Meggie Dillon.* It stood out against the dust, the loopy M and the plump D towering above the other letters.

Whap! A ball hit the roof of the car. Without thinking, I put up one hand as it bounced off. Too late. I turned to see two boys, one on each side of the street, playing catch over my head.

They must have been brothers; one was older than the

other, and taller, but they had the same face, and the same filthy shirts. I leaned forward to see what was pinned on the older one's shirt: a warty green pickle pin from the 1939 World's Fair. I had one at home, but I wouldn't wear it in a million years.

"Heads up," the pickle kid yelled, grabbing the ball; they darted away. At home I would have gone after them: *See my pinkie, see my thumb, see my fist, you'd better run*, but maybe eleven was too old for that here in Michigan.

Besides, Mom was outside again, looking as dusty as the car. She smiled when she saw my name, and reached out to write hers on the hood—most of it anyway, *Ingrid Dill*—

"After the war maybe they'll make bigger cars so I can fit my whole name." She patted the hood, leaving her handprint. "This poor old car won't go much more on these tires."

She didn't have to say the rest of what she was thinking. There wouldn't be any rubber for new ones until after the war. Rubber came from the Pacific, where some of our soldiers were fighting.

Mom went around the trunk to lift out a mess of clothes, last-minute things that hadn't fit into boxes. "How about some help?" she asked.

I trudged around to the back and pulled out the largest carton, in case those two idiot boys were watching. Let them see what they were up against. Back bent, I went up the walk with it.

Mom was bent over next to the front step, running her toe over a pile of dirt that could be a flower patch, except that there wasn't a lick of green.

What had I done with Grandpa's salad envelope?

Mom wiped her forehead. "It's as if someone strung a bunch of boxes together."

"Like those rabbit hutches we saw in upstate New York." I tried to smile. "And now we're the rabbits, I guess."

I spotted the boys again and made the worst face I could: nose up, lips pulled back over my teeth, tongue out—even better than the tan-mustache face.

I'd practiced it in the car's rearview mirror and even tried it out on Judy and Jiggs as they glared out from under the seat. The boys laughed, and I grinned back at them, an uneasy grin. *Grandpa, coffee cup to his mouth: "If your face freezes like that, Margaret . . ."*

I pushed the door of the rabbit hutch with one elbow and let myself in. I told myself I could hold on to the carton for one more second, long enough to slide it onto the scratched table that squatted on the linoleum floor. I wondered what was in it, heavy as lead. Jars of strawberry jam, probably; home-canned beans from last summer, green tomatoes and corn, and Grandpa's sweet pickles.

Enough was in that box to supply food for every single worker at that airplane factory, never mind just the three of us, Mom, Dad, and me.

Dad was rooting around somewhere in back. I craned my neck to see where he was . . .

. . . and the box slid out of my arms.

The noise was spectacular, an explosion of sound. Someone in one of the apartments must have thought so, too, from the way she screamed. Judy and Jiggs dived through the doorway into the back room to hide, and Mom, hands on her hips, stared down at the great shards of glass that were mixed in with the soupy mess of yellow and red. Her throat was moving. Was she going to cry?

"I'm sorry," I said. "I'm really sorry."

Dad stood in the doorway. "This is supper?" He glanced at Mom to see if she'd smile, but she was already pushing at the mess with a piece of shirt cardboard. She held up an unbroken jar. "Pickles!"

Grandpa's kitchen, the heat of it on a summer day, kettles bubbling on the stove, jars on the counters, the smell of vinegar, the air steamy. Eddie and I washed the cucumbers, and when we walked from the sink to the table, grains of sugar stuck to our feet.

Grandpa's pickles. Eddie loved them.

"I can clean up this mess," I told Mom.

She shook her head. "It's all right, baby. There's not room for both of us."

I tried to figure out what to do. "I'll get more boxes from the car." I stopped at the doorway as Dad leaned over and scooped Mom up by the elbows, dancing her around and singing: *"You get no bread with one meatball."*

Mom began to laugh, her bandana slipping so her ears showed. She reached up with one tomato-stained hand to touch his arm. "No gravy," she said, "no vegetables, no pickles."

Outside I sang under my breath, while across the street the boy with the pickle on his shirt made faces worse than mine.

Chapter Six

Late that afternoon I sat on the edge of the pullout couch in the living room. Stuffing was coming out of the arm, and it smelled a little like Grandpa's cellar. I was glad I didn't have to sleep on it.

I pulled out my entry forms from the Hot-O Soup Company. A can of tomato rice soup was drawn on top of each one. *The soup that keeps our servicemen going!* it said.

I looked out the window. I hoped Eddie had something better than tomato soup with lumps of rice to keep him going.

But I could win a hundred dollars here. I just had to write about something I'd do when the war was over. And the best part, I could send in as many entries as I wanted. Tons of them.

I knew what the soup people were dying to hear.

I picked up the pencil with the sharpest point and wrote: *As soon as the war is over, I'm going to heat up a cup of tomato rice soup. Delicious!*

Grandpa would say that was a big lie.

What would I really do?

I closed my eyes: *I'd be out on the roof, and I'd see Eddie walking along the gravel path. He'd look up and we'd both yell, and then I'd be flying through the house, calling Mom, calling Dad. . . .*

In back of me the radio blasted the news, something about spies in California. I shivered thinking about it. I was glad California was so far away.

I looked down at what I had written and changed part of it: *When the war is over and the soldiers come home, welcome them with a hot bowl of tomato rice soup. Delicious!*

Not a lie that way. Maybe some people liked tomato rice soup.

I pounded a stamp on front, leaving a smear of peanut butter across the edge. I was turning into Grandpa.

What next? I still had to tackle the last carton that held all my treasures. I went into the kitchen and slid it onto the table, watching the street outside through the window.

The two boys were there again, one of them trying to

climb a telephone pole. He'd probably be electrocuted by the time the war was over.

Dad was humming "Don't Sit Under the Apple Tree" under his breath while he fiddled around at the sink with a row of nails in his mouth.

"Nothing works," Mom said.

"Never mind," he said around the nails. "We're here. We're doing something for the war effort." He twisted a knob under the sink and rusty water spurted out of the faucet, hitting everything nearby: the red linoleum, a green cabinet, the leg of the scarred table.

"Good grief," a muffled voice yelled from the next apartment. "This place is going to be flooded again."

· "Oh, oh," Mom said.

"Not our fault—at least, I don't think so." Dad leaned forward to turn off the faucet with a wrenching sound. "And listen, the papers say that General Eisenhower is pushing his way past Normandy across France."

Wrong thing to say, I thought, seeing Mom's face.

Thousands of soldiers had been sent to France to land in Normandy, wave after wave of them, many shot by Germans as they came out of the water. June sixth, a warm sunny day, when I swam in the Atlantic for the first time this year!

Was it possible that Eddie was on the other side of that water in Normandy, zigzagging up that beach, carrying a rifle, pounding across the sand in heavy boots?

In Rockaway, Lily and I always kicked our shoes off on

the boardwalk so the sand wouldn't clump into them and weigh us down.

And carrying a rifle? How could he have managed that? Eddie was skinny. He'd be out of breath. He'd . . .

Don't think about that, I told myself. Still, I wondered what it was like in France. Sand like ours that looked like sugar? Green fields and lakes like the ones I had seen on the way to Willow Run?

Outside the window a thin stream of smoke from the factory rose up against a hazy yellow sky. Maybe France was like that, smoke from guns and tanks drifting toward the sky?

No, not like that. Eddie was having an adventure, too. *"Maybe I'm going to see Europe, Meg, the Rhine River and the Alps Mountains. You can sit at my place at the table. It's the best spot to see Rockaway."*

But now Rockaway seemed a million miles away, and Mom's eyes looked like Grandpa's the day we left.

Eddie's fault. All Eddie's fault.

He had come home that day last year, throwing his hat on the couch, telling me first.

"Just joined up, Meggie."

Mom glanced up from the white school socks she was knitting. "Joined up what?"

"The army, the infantry."

Mom's hand went to her cheeks, leaving finger marks.

"You're joking."

Eddie had lifted me in the air. "Going to win the war for you, Meg."

Mom dropped her needles onto her lap. "You're just eighteen."

"You're just doing that so Virginia Tooey will fall in love with your uniform," I told him.

"How did you guess?" he said, laughing.

Mom's eyes were closed. She spoke so low we could hardly hear her: "What have you done? How could you do that?"

Someone was pounding on the rabbit hutch door now. She didn't wait to be let in. "Ronnelle," she said. She was holding a toddler in rompers by the hand. "And little Lulu." She grinned. "After the comic strip *Lulu*. My husband, Michael, loves that."

I was sorry to see she had even more freckles than I did. Dad had always said mine would go away when I was grown.

Mom pushed out one of the rickety chairs for her to sit on, and I reached out with both arms for my treasure box and dumped it on the floor out of her way. Lulu was under the table now trying to grab Jiggs' tail.

"Can't stay," Ronnelle said. "Lulu will have your place destroyed in two minutes. She's like one of the B-24s I rivet together." She leaned forward to Dad and Mom. "Listen. When you turn the water on too fast, I get water, too."

Dad looked at her, shocked. "What kind of a thing is that?"

"Don't be sorry—the same thing happens to you when I turn on mine."

They talked about water and pipes for a while, all of them agreeing that they could hold out, it was a much easier time than the soldiers were having, and only for the duration anyway.

"My hair used to dip way down in front like the actress Veronica Lake," Ronnelle was saying. "But she doesn't wear it that way now. She said it was dangerous for the factory workers. So I don't either. All for the war effort." She bit her lip. "My husband, Michael, loved that peekaboo look."

I wondered if her husband loved her face with all those freckles.

I was sick of the war effort. I went over to lean against the screen.

"Michael's stationed at Peterborough Airport in England," she said, "flying thirty-five bombing missions before he comes home."

I looked over my shoulder to see Mom clicking her tongue against her teeth. "Thirty-five."

Ronnelle shook her head. "At first the casualty rate was eighty percent. Now it's a little better."

I tried to think of what she meant, but before I did, she went on. "Eight out of ten were killed on the missions."

I didn't want to think about that. From the window I watched the tough boy with the World's Fair pickle pinned to his shirt. He was hanging on to one of the telephone pole spikes; he probably thought he was King Kong. In one second he lost his grip and fell off. He bent over, staring at his knee, and dabbed at it with a yanked-up weed.

Disgusting.

"Six more missions to go," Ronelle said. "He hasn't even seen Lulu yet."

I heard a warning hiss from under the table: Jiggs the cat.

"I told you," Ronnelle said as I crawled underneath. By the time I pulled Lulu out she had a fistful of my hair clutched in her hand.

I took her with me, sliding the treasure box across the gritty floor and into the bedroom. I had written KEEP OUT! THIS MEANS U! all over the top and tied it with washline rope. It had enough knots to keep a Nazi spy busy for a couple of hours.

"Ho-nie-ko-doke!" I could hardly open it myself.

I loved that word, that almost word, *ho-nie-ko-doke*, from the Uncle Don Radio Show. "*Honie-ko-doke with an ala-ka-zon.*"

"Honey-doke," Lulu said, as if it were my name.

I had won a contest with Uncle Don: a bank with his picture. It didn't count, though. Everyone could win. All you had to do was send in a bunch of money. I wondered what I had done with that bank and the eleven cents I had tucked inside.

"Time to go," Ronnelle called.

"Bye, Honey," Lulu said, and toddled off. A few minutes

later, I found a knife in the kitchen, then hacked at the rope and the tape holding the top of the box until it snapped open.

The first treasure I saw was my old doll Rosemary Marjorie Anne. Some treasure. Rosemary was missing an arm and all the toes on one foot, and Judy, the mother cat, had been sick on her dress once, so she wasn't even wearing much in the way of clothes.

Underneath was the envelope Eddie had given me before he left, sealed up with Scotch tape. "We're going to open this together when I come home," he had said, top teeth on his lower lip, looking a little embarrassed.

"What is it?" I had asked.

"Well . . ." And then he had gone outside, not answering, probably on his way to Virginia Tooey's.

I held up the envelope, wondering how terrible it would be to open it and reseal it, but instead I tucked it far under my mattress and went back to my other treasures: shells and an abandoned duck's egg I had found at the beach. I had wrapped them in wads of toilet paper for safekeeping, but they were smashed to smithereens, with a bit of the yellow from the egg splotched across the edges.

I felt a lump in my throat thinking of Grandpa turning over a shell with his wide fingers. *"Do you know how old this must be, Margaret? Hundreds of years, sliding back and forth in the surf?"*

And now I had ruined them.

I stood up. From the bedroom I could see into the kitchen, and beyond that, the window. The tough kid had recovered from his fall. He marched up the street singing at the top of his lungs: *"Whistle while you work, Hitler is a jerk. . . ."*

I reached for the other stuff in the box: old contest entries, a postcard collection I had started with only two postcards, and a few pennies in the bottom. And something else. Grandpa's envelope of salad seeds. I ran my fingers over the words: *lettuce, cukes, tomatoes.*

I could see Grandpa's face as he handed me the envelope. And then I realized it had come unglued and the seeds were scattered over the bottom of the box. All useless now.

I was glad Grandpa was so far away. He'd never know what had happened to them.

> *Dear Lily,*
>
> *There is no ocean here at Willow Run, no paint on the houses. They go together in a row and you can hear people talking and fighting and even going to the bathroom. The houses were just slapped up because thousands of people have come here to make the bombers. My father took me in to see. The factory is a mile long. Everyone just makes one little piece that they fit*

together until the B-24 is finished. My father says they build a bomber every 103 minutes. I hate the whole thing. How is the attic? Did you find the red candy?

Margaret

Chapter Seven

I had forgotten to tell Lily: the bedroom was so dark at night I might have been locked in a trunk. Not even a window!

In that skinny bed I kept thinking of my yellow room in Rockaway. The window there was always propped open, and I could smell the sea, could tell the difference between high tide and low: that clean-washed smell as the water rose, the smell of grit and sand when it ebbed. And always the sound of seagulls screeching.

I remembered listening to the boom of the surf and figuring out what I'd do the next day. Sometimes it was swimming with Lily, or going out in the boat. Maybe it was even the movies with Grandpa. I hated to go to the movies with Grandpa.

He'd whisper through the whole thing, grabbing my arm. *Vatch out, mister. He's coming up the stairs and he's got a gun. More popcorn, Margaret?*

I turned over now, looking for the thin line of light that came in under my door from the kitchen.

Dad was getting ready to go to work on the night shift— the graveyard shift, he called it—and outside, a door slammed: Ronnelle on her way out, too.

I stretched my arms and spread my fingers like the starfish that drifted near the jetties in Rockaway, their spiny arms floating just under the surface of the green water. I could touch one wall the same way, and drift a couple of inches to touch the other.

Somewhere there was a sound. A cough?

I took a quick breath. Was someone hiding under the bed? The newscaster had been talking about spies, but they were in California, I thought, or was it Florida?

I tried to see in that dark room, holding my eyes open, trying not to blink. We were on top of the largest plane factory in the world. Wouldn't there be spies? Wouldn't there be people who wanted to know how the planes were made?

Or worse yet, to blow them up?

I remembered a movie Grandpa and I had seen. In the end the movie spy had dropped all the way from the top of the Statue of Liberty into the water below. But that was after he had ruined half the country.

I swung my head and shoulders over the edge of the bed even though it was too dark to see, and there it was again, a cough. But then I realized. It wasn't from this apartment, it was from the other side of the wall, in the apartment next to us, but not on Ronnelle's side.

I shimmied back up, leaning close to the bars of the bed, and heard a man's voice, and then the woman's. She was still coughing. A boy was there, too, his voice loud and high. No, I heard the difference. Two boys.

Those tough kids?

Just a family, then, not spies at all. I could feel the relief in my chest; it was almost as if I were beginning to breathe. They began talking all at once, and before I could stop myself I rapped on the wall with my knuckles.

"What was that?" one of the boys asked. He sounded nervous.

Then the father's voice: "It was nothing. Nothing at all. We're safe."

And the mother in her soft throat-clearing voice: "We're here together. Don't worry."

A cottage in the Catskill Mountains one weekend. Was I five, six? We had shared one room, Mom and Dad in the big bed against the window, Eddie and I in cots. All together. Safe.

"I want to go home," the same boy said. "Right now. Home to my apartment in Detroit."

"Baby Kennis," said the other one.

"Harlan," said the mother, warning him.

Harlan and Kennis.

It was too late to take back the rap on the wall. I lay there, turning the pillow over to make it cooler, and thought of Grandpa again.

I wondered what he was doing. He used to come to our house every morning, a mess of greens for Mom under one arm, his tackle box and a greasy-looking bag of lunch in the other. *"I suppose you want to go fishing, Margaret. I'll take you if you can manage to keep from talking all the time."*

"No, thanks. There's something else I have to do. Lily and I have plans."

I had said that at least once a week.

Maybe I should have gone with him all the time. Never mind. Eddie was his favorite. He didn't need me there every two minutes.

I closed my eyes. Was I going to cry over Grandpa? Grandpa, who smelled of pickle vinegar and mixed up his *v*s and *w*s?

Certainly not.

On the other side of the wall the boys were making a lot of noise, fighting with each other, knocking into things. One of them must have turned over a chair. I could feel the vibration on the iron bed bars against my head.

"That's enough," the mother said.

I'd never get to sleep.

Another chair went over.

Without thinking, I reached up and rapped against the wall again.

For a moment, there was silence; then someone banged back with a fist. A hard bang. Not a kid's bang. It must have been the father. He kept banging.

I slid my face under my doll Rosemary's fat cloth body, where I couldn't see anything, not even that skinny light under the door. And then the two cats jumped up on the bed with me and Mom stood at the door. "Who's doing that?"

I came out from under Rosemary as Mom turned on the overhead light. The string with its knob on the end swayed back and forth, making line shadows on the wall.

One of the boys was banging, too, now, his fist lighter than the father's.

Mom sat on the edge of the bed next to me. "What nerve." She put her head close to the wall. "That's enough in there."

Something was growing inside my chest again, something so big it felt as if I couldn't get my breath, as if I were going to explode. I sat up in bed and then my breath did come, and I was crying, crying loud enough for them to hear me on the other side of the wall.

I kept telling myself to stop as Mom put her arms around me and began to rock back and forth, as the mother on the other side of the wall said, "Ah, ah."

"What is it?" Mom kept asking.

"I don't know." I was barely able to get the words out.

How could I tell her it was Grandpa's pickle jars broken on the kitchen floor when I had watched him seal the tops, his head bent over, humming under his breath?

How could I say it was Eddie, who had sung "Marching Along Together" with me in the Catskill Mountains when I was five? Or that I was glad when Eddie left because I thought it would be fun to be the only one home?

How could I say that I had thought this was going to be the best adventure anyone could have?

"We'll go home when the war is over," Mom said.

"Amen," the father said on the other side of the wall.

"We'll have a wonderful party, and Eddie will be home, and we'll row out in the bay on a sunny day," Mom said, smoothing back my hair.

"There's not even a tree here." My voice was thick. "No cucumbers. Nothing."

Dad stood in the doorway, shaking his head.

I gulped and stopped crying. I knew he had to go to work. After a while they went back into the kitchen. I whispered to the wall. "Sorry," I said. "Sorry." But I didn't say it loud enough for anyone to hear.

I gave Jiggs and Judy a pat and closed my eyes. *Go to sleep,* I told myself, and then right next to me, I heard a knocking: three quick bings and a bong.

My eyes flew open. This wasn't from the tough boys' wall

at the head of the bed. These bings came from my right side—or was it my left? I could never tell the difference between left and right.

It wasn't from Ronnelle's apartment. That wall was next to the kitchen and Mom and Dad's bedroom.

"Hey," I said aloud. Suddenly I knew exactly what it meant. I'd heard it on the radio a million times, the army's code: V for Victory.

I scrunched over to the wall: bing bing bing bong, I went with my knuckles.

After a moment, the code came again.

I couldn't wait until morning when I'd find out who was in that apartment in back of us.

Chapter Eight

I threw on my clothes and ate cornflakes leaning over the sink, half the milk dripping onto my blouse. I wiped myself off and tiptoed outside to investigate.

I had to count: our apartment was the fourth from the corner, so what I had to do was go around the block, count down four apartments, and . . . pretty good figuring. If the war lasted another seven years or so, I could sign up as a secret agent.

I swung my arms and practiced whistling, which was still at a kindergarten baby level, marching off and on the curb to let the grown-ups pass on their way to work at the factory.

And there on the corner was the ice cream man and his

truck. He looked as grumpy as he had the first time I'd seen him, so I narrowed my eyes into tiny slits at him.

He narrowed his eyes right back and took himself to the other side of the truck, where I couldn't see him. But he wanted to laugh, I could see that. It was just the way it was in school. Something funny would happen and Sister Martha's eyes would shoot lightning like Flash Gordon. "Stop acting like hyenas," she'd say.

That always made me laugh harder. *Hyenas.* And sometimes I thought Sister Martha's lips were twitching, too.

I looked back over my shoulder now, but the ice cream man had forgotten me already. He locked the door of the SUNDAE, MONDAY, AND ALWAYS truck, bent down, and put the key under the fender.

And then I was around the corner, counting apartments, and there was a freckle-faced girl with messy hair in front of the fourth one, the jump-roper I had seen the other day. She was slapping a washline up and down and jumping faster than I'd ever seen anyone do it in Rockaway . . . and with bare feet.

She was so tough!

Without thinking I took a few running steps toward her, rocked back and forth, and then I was in with her, jumping a thousand times a minute, both of us shouting as the rope whistled around us.

I knew I was going to miss; my heart was pounding: "*. . . thirty, forty . . .*"

We collapsed on the curb, hardly able to talk. "Bing bing bing bong," I managed.

She grinned at me. "V for Victory. I think you scared Harlan and Kennis. Good for them."

"Hyenas," I said, thinking they had scared me a lot more than I had scared them.

She rolled up her pants legs to her knees. "See these scars?" she asked between breaths. "Fell off a seesaw. Ten stitches. Didn't even cry. My real name is Janie. Everyone calls me Patches now."

Ten stitches. "Brave." I'd have been howling if the doctor had come near me with a needle and thread. "I know you're tough, not even bothering to wear shoes." I tried to think of something interesting to tell her. "I'm Meggie. I just made a horrible face at that ice cream man."

"People say he's a spy," Patches said. "He is so mean."

"He certainly is. He keeps his key under the truck. Kids could come along and have a zillion ice cream cups if they wanted to."

She stared at me, her forehead dotted with perspiration, and began to grin. "Let's just take a look. . . ."

"Let's."

She looped the rope over her arm and threw it on the bare patch of dirt in front of her apartment; then we dashed down the block, turned the corner, and almost ran into the boy with the World's Fair pickle. Harlan or Kennis.

"Have to take up the whole sidewalk, Harlan?" Patches asked.

Harlan.

"It's a free country," he said. "I was just going to buy myself some ice cream from Arnold the Spy." He swiped at his face, leaving a trail of dirt on his cheek. "He should be in the army."

"My brother's in the army," I said. "Eddie. He's a hero."

"That's nothing," Harlan said. "My uncle Leo was, too. He's dead. Shot at Palermo."

I looked at him, horrified, telling myself that would never happen to Eddie. Eddie was probably home on leave with Grandpa anyway.

We walked back toward the ice cream truck. A lot more happened here in Willow Run than at home, I thought. Ten stitches, dead uncles . . . and so I reached under the ice cream truck, groping along the sandy tire until I found the key and held it up over my head like a trophy.

Harlan stared at me. "Wow."

And Patches: "Meggie's not afraid of anything."

Before I knew it I had put the key into the lock. I opened the little square door in the truck and put my face into the misty air as it swirled out. Inside, ice cream bars and Dixie cups were stacked on top of each other, and rows of wooden spoons were lined up like slats on a wood fence.

"I have orange ice pops on special today," I said.

"I'll take one," said Harlan, but Patches shook her head. "Too cold for me."

I reached inside and pulled out two pops, seeing Eddie's face, and Grandpa's, and even Lily Mollahan's. I didn't have to wonder what they'd think. I *knew* what they'd say. I picked up a stone, my heart fluttering. Why was I doing this? "We'll put two scratches in the running board," I said, "and pay him back."

Harlan nodded. "Good idea. That way we won't go to jail if we get caught." He bit his lip. "If we get caught, we won't go to jail. Arnold the Spy will probably shoot us."

Quickly I made two marks on the running board and shoved the key back on top of the tire. Then we ran as fast as we could, away from the truck, up the block, around the corner, to sit on the curb in front of Patches' apartment and eat the pops.

The sweetness was on my tongue and in my throat, but somehow it didn't taste right. Then, a few minutes after we'd finished, Arnold the Spy walked by. I wished I had never taken the pop.

I'd pay him back the minute I got my allowance.

Chapter Nine

Patches and I were making up a code. One knock for A, two knocks for B, all the way through the alphabet. It took forever to get two words out.

It was the middle of the afternoon; I was hot as a biscuit leaning against the wall in that bedroom. And then suddenly, in my ear, Patches shouted, "Gotta go now. Have to buy school shoes. My mom says they're on sale."

"But it's just the beginning of summer," I yelled back. And then I realized: I could actually hear her, even though the noise was muffled. It was a bit of a disappointment after all that knocking.

From the kitchen, Mom called me in a loud whisper.

"Meggie? People are trying to sleep after working on the night shift."

I took myself out on the stoop, seeing a million people walking back and forth, but no Harlan, then had to watch a column of ants carrying crumbs from one spot to another because there wasn't one thing in the world to do. If Grandpa had been there we would have done something, I knew that, even though I couldn't imagine what it would have been. *"The thing is to do something, Margaret. Carpe diem."*

I tried to remember what that meant. Seize the day, was it? Grandpa always said that.

The ants weren't carrying crumbs; they were dragging a dead Japanese beetle around. I wondered if they were going to eat it or bury it.

On the other side of me, the door banged open. Ronnelle came down the steps, Lulu straddling her hip, sucking her thumb.

"Ah, the flood girl." Ronnelle came to a stop. "What are you doing?" Before I could answer, she snapped her fingers "Meggie, right?"

I nodded.

"You're doing nothing," she said. "Come to the movies with us. It's air-cooled. Perfect for today."

Lulu raised her hand. "Honey-doke," she said, smiling at me with crooked white teeth.

"If we're lucky we'll be the only ones in the movie this early," Ronnelle said. "Lulu can crawl up and down the aisle playing hi-ho Silver, and I can watch Abbott and Costello in peace for two minutes." She shook her head, yawning. "I work at night, and a woman a few doors down babysits while I'm gone. There's not much sleep for me."

I stood up, waving at Lulu. Why not go to the movie? I thought. *Carpe diem*. I pushed open the kitchen door with one hand. Mom was fiddling around with stuff on the counter. "How about I go to the movies?"

Mom glanced over her shoulder, her mouth open, looking uneasy.

"Not alone," I said quickly, "with Ronnelle. *Carpe diem*."

"You sound like Grandpa." She smiled, reached over to the table for her tan change purse, and snapped it open. "Pay your own way."

Outside we went down one block and up the next, all of them identical. If you ever got lost, you'd really be in trouble, I thought.

"We have to hurry," Ronnelle said, lugging Lulu on one hip as Lulu leaned back to look at the cement, the street, and a sparrow winging overhead.

It was a relief to reach the movie, dark and cool, to sit halfway down with cups of hot popcorn—a thousand times better than sitting on the stoop watching ants hold a funeral service for a beetle.

"Ah," Ronnelle said, putting Lulu on the floor. "My husband Michael loves the movies. He laughs and laughs."

I could see the brightness in her eyes. "I miss him,

Meggie. I've known him since we were in high school. Six more missions! If only he's all right, then he's home, and we'll begin our lives again."

I nodded. She wasn't much older than Eddie, I thought, but I was too shy to ask.

"Miss him, Honey-doke."

There was something I did ask. "You have a lot of freckles," I said, as if that weren't a bad thing, as if everyone wanted a million blots covering their face . . . as if I didn't mind that I had freckles.

Ronnelle laughed. "I used to think I looked horrible, but Michael . . ." She hesitated. "He thinks I look like that movie star, Katharine Hepburn."

I sat back watching, laughing as Abbott and Costello came onto the screen, fighting. Lulu called "Hi-ho" a half-dozen times, then climbed onto Ronnelle's lap to fall asleep. Ronnelle put her head back and slept, too.

For the first time I thought it might not be so bad to have those freckles, not so terrible that everyone in school called me Freckle Face.

The war news began: pictures of soldiers against a gray stone wall in a place called Sainte Mere-Eglise, tired, filthy, sitting there in the mud, heads bent, legs stretched in front of them as the rain poured down.

I remembered Eddie getting ready for his dates with Virginia Tooey, his hair slicked back, still wet, so you could see the comb marks running through it. He spent hours in front of the bathroom mirror, while I banged on the door yelling that he was taking forever.

On the screen the scene changed and a line of soldiers marched along a road. They grinned at the camera, shoving each other a little. One of them had a wreath of daisies wound around his helmet.

Was it Eddie? I sat up straight, watching his back go down the road. Thin, like Eddie, feet slopping along in boots. My heart flip-flopped in my chest. *Could it be?*

Ronnelle was awake now, pointing as the camera zeroed in on a huge basket of mail that was being hoisted over the side of a ship to the waiting sailors. "I write to Michael every day," she said. "Twice a day sometimes. He writes me, too, but sometimes I have to wait weeks, then it all arrives in a bunch."

I nodded as I watched a woman cook a pot of something she said was full of nourishment but didn't take a lot of rationed meat. That was what Mom always said about Spam with Grandpa's pickles. But this looked even more dreadful.

"Time to go, kids," Ronnelle said, smoothing back Lulu's hair.

We marched out. I thought about the soldier on the screen with daisies on his helmet.

My brother, Eddie. Could it have been?

Dear Grandpa,

Thanks for the letters you keep sending. I'm glad your garden is growing. I miss fishing with you, too.

I may have seen Eddie in the movies.

Love,

Meggie

P.S. You asked about the salad garden. I haven't quite started it yet.

Notes for Hot-O Soup:

When the war is over . . .

1. . . . we'll have a party with fireworks that will light up all of Rockaway.

2. . . . I won't eat Spam for the rest of my life. I'll try Hot-O Soup instead.

3. . . . I'll put real butter on everything, even a lump in Hot-O Soup.

4. . . . I will never take anything I should pay for.

Chapter Ten

I lay sideways across the bed. "Here." I tapped on the wall with my fingers.

"Right," said a ghostly voice from the other side of the wall.

"Meggie?" Mom called from the kitchen. "Why don't you go outside and get some fresh air?"

"Nothing to do out there."

Sawing sounds came from the other side; I picked up my knife and began to saw, too, until there was a tiny hole.

"Watch out." Patches' voice was clearer now. "You're going to stab me with that."

"It's just a butter knife from the kitchen. It doesn't even cut butter." I leaned back. It might not cut butter, but plaster was crumbling, the hole growing, and light beamed through from the other side. "Enough," I told her. "You don't want the whole wall to fall down."

Laughing, she stuck her finger through the hole and wiggled it around like a pale snake.

"Let me see," I said.

She pulled her finger away and I peered through into her bedroom. It was exactly the same as mine but there wasn't as much stuff thrown around; her new brown school shoes were on the table next to her bed.

She leaned forward until I could see the flecks of green in her brown eyes. "This is going to be terrific," she said. "We don't have to yell one bit, we can talk all night long if we want."

Mom's footsteps tapped down the hallway, and I rolled off the bed, glancing back over my shoulder to be sure she couldn't see the hole.

"It's dark in here. Miserable." Mom dumped a pile of clean underwear on my bed. "I want you to go outside, make some friends. *Do something.*"

I wondered if she could hear Patches breathing. "All right." I shoved the underwear under the bed so Patches wouldn't see it. "I have to mail letters anyway."

I skipped out the door, hearing Mom sigh, "I just washed all that."

As I went down the street I looked back; there was a blue star in Ronnelle's window for her husband, and one in ours for Eddie. I saw Patches coming as I turned the corner. I waved a pile of envelopes at her: a letter to Grandpa, four Hot-O Soup entries, and a quick twenty-five-words-or-less contest I had entered . . . *Why I Like Sparkling Blue.*

Just then a ball whizzed by me so fast I could feel the breeze lift my hair.

Harlan: filthy shorts, scabby knees, the World's Fair pickle pinned to his striped shirt, and a white bag under his arm. "Can't you even catch?" His sweaty face was streaming. He raised his shirt and swiped at his chin, leaving a sooty mark across the stripes.

Sparkling Blue makes your clothes white, even Harlan's, I thought, grinning to myself, and then I got a better look at the bag in his arms. So did Patches, who had just caught up to me, her bare feet as filthy as Harlan's shirt. "You stole more ice cream, Harlan Tucker."

"Did not," he said. "I come from a family of heroes, not thieves." He put the bag down on the ground. "I'm going to show you two something." He pulled a dollar bill out of his pocket, as filthy as his shirt. "This doesn't count as money, of course. I'd never spend it in a million years. My uncle Leo gave it to me before he went overseas."

Patches leaned forward. "The one who was . . ."

"Shot. Right. This is all I have left of him."

Patches and I took a quick look at each other; neither of us knew what to say.

"He won't be coming home to Detroit. He wanted to

start a hardware store there when the war ended," Harlan said. "He said we could be partners and I should hold on to this dollar bill until he got back."

Like Eddie with the envelope. I raised my hand to brush back my bangs. *No, not like that at all.*

"I'm going to have a hardware store myself someday so I can remember him," Harlan said. "I'll never use this dollar, though. Never."

I shook my head. "No."

"Anyway," he said. "I dug six scratches into Arnold the Spy's running board. I'll pay the whole thing back someday. That's what Leo would want me to do."

"Six?" How could he have done that? I was terrible at math; I couldn't even figure out how much money that would be.

"Yup. Two each. It's going to be a scorcher today."

My mouth watered, but at the same time I felt a lurch in my chest. What would Grandpa say? What would Eddie say? And Lily Mollahan would never steal ice cream, even though the ice cream man might be a spy.

All my fault. I should never have told them about the key. If only I hadn't done that.

Harlan held out the bag. "I don't think . . . ," I began, then sighed. "I'll take the strawberry."

Patches shook her head. "My mother made ice-cube pops."

We sat on the curb eating two ice creams each, and then we ate the ones for Patches, too. I could feel an uneasiness in my stomach. "They taste stale or something," I said.

"I wouldn't put it past him," Harlan said. "Secondhand ice cream."

"Don't be ridiculous," Patches said. I could see she had no patience for Harlan.

Harlan wiped his mouth with his shirt again. "That's done," he said. "Now what?"

"Mailbox," Patches said.

Harlan took the envelopes from my hand and fanned them out. "What's this stuff?"

"You're not supposed to read other people's mail," Patches said, looking over his shoulder.

"Contests," I said reluctantly. They'd probably think I was crazy.

"No," Harlan said. "This one. Josef von Frisch? *Von?*"

I hesitated. "My grandfather."

"A Nazi?"

"No." I shook my head. "Certainly not."

"Sounds German to me."

I took a breath. "Mongolian."

"Where's that?" Patches asked.

"Australia," I said.

Harlan bent down to scratch a mosquito bite on his leg. "The mailbox is a couple of blocks down."

I nodded. I had no idea where Mongolia was. Geography was harder than math. I had gotten a D on the last map quiz just before school closed.

I followed them down the street, past a long line of apartment houses with rows of trailers between them, metallic gray and round, like turtles dozing on logs, and dropped the envelopes in the mail, crossing my fingers over the entries.

We wandered back toward my apartment, passing the ice cream truck.

"He moves the truck every day or so, looking for top-secret secrets, I guess," Harlan said. "He probably keeps them frozen inside the truck somewhere."

"It's going to take us a hundred years to get back to the apartment if we keep stopping every two minutes," Patches said.

They began to argue, but I was thinking. What could I do about Arnold the Spy and paying him back? How could I ever ask Dad for the money? What would he think if he knew I had stolen two—no, three, ice creams, and because it was my fault, if you really counted them all it was eight or nine.

Patches began to say something else, then stopped walking. I nearly bumped into her.

A mud-colored jeep was parked in front of our apartment. Harlan grabbed my shoulder with his sticky hand. "Someone's in trouble."

Ahead of us two women were standing frozen on the corner. They reached out to hold hands.

"They've come with a telegram," he said. "Probably someone's missing or maybe killed in action."

It seemed as if everything inside began to slide from my head down into my chest, into my stomach. My legs didn't feel as if they would hold me up. "I think I'd better go in now."

I waited to run until I was nearly up the path; then I stumbled up the step and went inside.

> *Dear Eddie,*
>
> *I'm sending this letter even though they say you're missing in action. I know you'll be found by the time it gets there. In fact, I'm sure I saw you in the movie I went to the other day.*
>
> *Please write as soon as you're found. Mom and Dad are crying.*
>
> *Love,*
>
> *Meggie*
>
> *P.S. I thought about opening your envelope, but I guess not. We're going to open it together, right?*

Chapter Eleven

I had to go to the movies. I couldn't remember the way Ronnelle had taken me, but I didn't want to knock on her door.
She would have asked me to come in.

She had spent the last hour in our kitchen, chopping
vegetables and chunks of pork fat into a soup that simmered
in a pot on the stove, a soup that no one would eat, but she
had whispered, "Have to have food, sooner or later."

Something was wrong with my mouth; my lips were
numb, so I couldn't talk the way I usually did.

I went across the bare packed earth in front of the rabbit
hutch and down the block. I managed the first few streets,
then stopped to ask a boy on a bicycle. "The movie?"

The boy pointed. In my mind I kept repeating the directions he gave me: *"Two blocks, then left; one block, then left again."* Who cared if someone saw me and thought I was talking to myself?

I had money in my pocket. I had taken it off the kitchen table, the newspaper boy's money; it was more than enough. I was probably going to end up in jail someday, but this was different from the Arnold the Spy money. I could pay the paper boy as soon as I got my allowance on Wednesday. I could even tell him that myself. He looked patient, kind of like a sparrow, with those skinny legs and no chin.

It made me smile. I'd have to tell Eddie that.

And then I realized. I had forgotten for a second. I might not ever see Eddie again.

But the movie. Maybe everything would be all right after all. It might be the same movie, the same news I had seen with Ronnelle. I'd take a look at the soldier with the daisies on his helmet again. And this time I'd be sure it was Eddie.

Please let it be Eddie. I'll never take ice cream again. I'll never eat ice cream again. I'd even ask Dad for the money. I wouldn't wait for my allowance.

Dad at the kitchen table holding Mom's hand.

I didn't want to think about that. Instead, I thought of Pathe News and Eddie on the movie screen. I wouldn't wait for the second feature. I'd go home, running all the way; I'd go into that kitchen with the scratched-up table and tell them.

Would Mom be sitting there, her round face milk-bottle white? Still not talking, her fingers pleating her handkerchief? Dad next to her saying everything was going to be all right, like the song, *"We'll meet again,"* but with tears dripping from his chin?

I saw him, I'd say. *He isn't missing in action. He was marching along with a bunch of soldiers, wearing daisies on his helmet. He's right there in Normandy, France.*

Those daisies. It made perfect sense. Eddie loved gardening the way Grandpa and I did, the way Mom and Dad did. I came from a family of gardeners the way Harlan said he came from a family of heroes.

Half a block in back of me, a voice: "Meggie?"

It was Patches. She didn't say anything, just began to walk along next to me, but she knew. I knew she knew. Harlan came next. "Hey, wait up." He had another Dixie cup in his hand. I was losing count of how many ice creams he'd taken, but I couldn't worry about that now.

"Do you have to follow us everywhere?" Patches said.

"She needs every friend she's got," Harlan said. "That's what my mother said when Uncle Leo . . . you know."

Harlan's face was covered with beads of sweat. But even though I could feel the sun on my head, I was shivering, icy cold as if it were the middle of winter and I had forgotten my coat. I folded my arms across my chest, wishing I had a blanket to wrap around my shoulders.

"Where are you going?" he asked.

"To the movies." My lips were still numb.

"The movies?" He sounded surprised. "Anyway, wrong way, wrong time," he said. "The movie isn't supposed to open for another hour or so anyway."

"Show me where it is. I'll get there early and just wait."

He finished the last of his Dixie cup and tossed it in the street. "I got Veronica Lake again," he said.

What was he talking about?

"On the Dixie cup lid. I already have her twice. I'm looking for Gary Cooper."

"Where's the movie?" I asked.

He chewed his lip. "Got any extra money?"

"A few cents."

"That'll do it," he said. "I'll go with you." He reached down to pick up a stick.

"I'll go, too," Patches said, hopping on one foot. "Stones all over the place. But I can pay my own way."

I kept thinking of the two soldiers in the kitchen, their hats off. One of them looked as if he might be sick. A piece of paper, the telegram, was on the table, and everyone was staring at it.

"Missing in action . . . June sixth . . . Normandy . . . Possible that he's still alive."

One of the soldiers had said that. It must be true. Of course it was true.

If only I could go back to the apartment for a sweater, but how could I walk past Mom and Dad at the kitchen table?

"There's the movie." Harlan ran the stick along the ground after him, raising dust and making a *swish-swish* noise. "In Detroit we sneak into the movies all the time."

I tried to listen to him. Lily did that, too. But I kept thinking of the words in my head: *missing in action.* What a terrible sound that had.

"We can sit right here on the curb and wait for the woman to go into the ticket booth." Harlan slid down against the telephone pole to sit on the ground.

"Will you stop talking?" Patches asked him. "You're vibating in my ears."

I sank down next to them, watching Harlan make circles in the soft dusty earth with his stick.

After a while a woman went into the ticket booth. I watched her arrange everything: a money box, a pile of blue tickets, smoothing back her long pageboy hairdo.

"We're in luck," Harlan said. "She's earlier than I thought."

We went into the empty theater. I was glad they were with me. Somehow it would have been terrible to be alone there in the dark.

Just before the picture started, someone else came in. Harlan nudged me as the person went down the aisle. "There's Arnold the Spy."

I shook my head. "We should never have taken that ice cream."

"What's he doing watching a movie anyway?" Harlan

whispered. "He should be in the army, overseas somewhere, like my uncle Leo was."

I couldn't say *like my brother*. I wished Eddie weren't in the army, wished we were all home. *Fishing with Grandpa, the backs of my legs against the rough rocks of the jetty, the water swishing up, cooling my feet, my ankles.*

I wished the war were over. No, I wished it had never started.

I didn't want to be the only one at home. How had I ever thought that would be fun?

The picture began, and I tried to pay attention. *It's an ordinary day,* I told myself. *I'm watching this boy from Iowa on the screen and he's on a train going into the army. And then I'm going to see the news . . . and what a surprise. Eddie will be marching along on the screen—and everyone thought he was missing! See? Nothing to it.* I shouldn't have even written that two-minute letter to him. By the time it reached him, he would have forgotten he had even been missing.

It was hard to pay attention, though. It seemed to take forever until the boy from Iowa was wearing an army uniform and it was over.

At last I heard the music that meant the news was coming next. The picture grew large on the screen.

But it wasn't the same news I had seen with Ronnelle. There were soldiers, but they weren't marching; they sat in a muddy field, one of them drinking from a canteen, another with his head back against a stone wall, sleeping.

Not one of them had daisies on his helmet. Not one of them was Eddie.

The camera switched and a line of girls marched along a platform in white bathing suits. They made me think about Virginia Tooey. What would she think when she didn't get letters from Eddie anymore?

The cartoon began. I closed my eyes, listening to Elmer Fudd sputtering over something Bugs Bunny had done. By the time I opened them again, Elmer had a rifle. He was chasing Bugs up and down a pile of rounded hills and into the woods.

And a sign wrote itself across the screen in huge white letters: THAT'S ALL, FOLKS.

Maybe there were woods in France. You could get lost in the woods and wander around for a while before you found your way out. Of course you could.

And then I realized I couldn't remember what Eddie looked like.

How could that be?

And then I quieted myself. Lily had the key to our house in Rockaway. Everything was still there: the couch in the living room, the lamp Mom had gotten for her birthday two years ago, the picture of Eddie in his uniform smiling at us.

As soon as I could make myself go back into the kitchen of our rabbit hutch, I'd write to Lily and ask her to send his picture.

"I have to go home," I told them.

"Don't you want to see the second feature? It's a western," Harlan said.

I shook my head and stood up. Patches stood with me.

Harlan waved his hand. "I'm going to stay until the end, otherwise we're wasting all this money."

Patches and I walked out of the movie, blinking in the light. I began to hurry when I heard someone in back of us, whistling "Saturday Night (Is the Loneliest Night of the Week)."

Eddie used to sing that on his way out the door to go to the movies with Virginia Tooey. But I knew he didn't think it was lonely. He would pat the top of my head as he went by and do a little dance down the steps.

"What are you thinking about?" Patches asked.

I shook my head. If I told her, I knew I'd begin to cry.

Chapter Twelve

I said, "See you later," to Patches and went into the kitchen. No one was there. A cup was on its side at the table, a lake of milky tea spread out beside it and dripping onto the floor. I dipped my finger into it: not even warm. It had been there a long time.

"Nothing like a hot cup of tea to soothe the spirit," Grandpa always said; and Ronelle: *"Have to have food sooner or later."*

I tiptoed to Mom and Dad's bedroom door. Their room was almost as small as mine, the double bed taking up most of the space. A tall floor lamp with a ripped shade leaned against the wall.

In the dim light I could see Mom lying under the patch-work quilt, her arm hanging off the side, the crumpled handkerchief in her hand. I backed away, thinking she had gone to sleep, but she turned and sat up. She wasn't crying anymore, but her eyes were swollen, and a strand of hair was stuck to her cheek. "Oh, baby, where have you been?" Her voice was breathless. "We didn't know where you were."

I started to say I wasn't the baby anymore, but that would have made it worse. "I'm sorry."

"Dad is out looking for you. How could you do that?"

I couldn't say I had gone to the movies. How would that have sounded?

"Go outside, look for Dad. He's frantic trying to find you."

I didn't move.

"I thought . . . ," she began, and stopped. "Two gone in a day." She sank back on the bed again, her eyes closed, and tears seeped out from under her lashes. "Go find Dad," she whispered.

I went through the kitchen then, turning the teacup upright before I went outside.

I heard Dad's whistle when I opened the door, a shrill sound that he used to call me home for dinner when I was at the beach.

"I'm here," I called, going down the cement walk. Kennis was sitting there trying to stick two pieces of wood together with a couple of rubber bands.

Dad stood in the middle of the street, his back to me,

whistling again. I kept calling and waving as I went toward him until he turned and saw me.

"Meggie?"

"I'm sorry," I said again, but he pulled me to him, hugging me so hard I had trouble taking a breath. I knew he'd ask where I had been, so I rushed on. "Listen, I could make more tea. Some for you and some for Mom. Lots of sugar."

His eyes were red.

My father crying.

"What happened to you?" he asked.

I stared down at the cracked cement under my feet. "I was with Harlan and Patches," I said slowly. "The kids on the other side of the walls."

Dad nodded. "It's all right. We were just worried. . . ." He swallowed hard. He was having trouble with his mouth, too.

"Let's go home," I said. "Let's just go home to Rockaway. Eddie won't even know how to picture us here. He won't know what it's like."

Dad closed his eyes for a moment; then we walked along the street together. "I want to show you something," he said.

He took long steps, so I had to hurry to keep up with him. We passed a row of ugly apartment houses, then a bunch of trailers with wash strung on lines from one to the other. People were coming and going from the factory, swinging their lunch pails.

And then the houses were gone, and the people, and we

walked along a dirt road toward open fields. "It's just a little farther," Dad said.

As the road curved, I saw what he wanted me to see: a row of trees that hadn't been sawed away, and after that a field of grass so high we could just about see over it.

I stood there breathing in that dusty air; then I reached out with my fingers to touch the feathery top of a yellow plant. The sound of insects buzzing was everywhere, a sleepy sound like the one I always heard when I went around the back of Grandpa's house into his garden.

One day Eddie hammered thin stakes into the ground and twirled the tiny bean vines around them. "What would I do without you, Edvard?" Grandpa said.

Above, the sun was a glowing ball lighting a path through the field so the green stalks in the center were blurred. It was almost as if I could walk across the top of them and keep on walking straight up into the sky. And at the far end of the field was a small house, unpainted, with a tiny porch in front, and a stone chimney that leaned a little. It looked as if it had been there forever.

"Willow Run. It was all like this before the war," Dad said. "A small town named for a stream that ran through here long ago . . . trees, everything green and lovely."

He waved his hand in front of him. "Maybe it will be like that again afterwards." He shook his head. "Europe in ruins. Monte Cassino, that beautiful cathedral, hundreds of years old, gone. You know, Meggie, it's all because people haven't learned to get along with each other. Jews gone because they were Jews. Old people because they were old."

I felt my breath catch. Grandpa was old. "Grandpa would love this," I said.

"I thought that, too, the other day, when I saw it for the first time." Dad tilted his head. "I don't know why, but I keep thinking about that summer we went to the Catskill Mountains. August. The days were warm, but we could feel the beginning of fall in the air."

I squeezed my eyes shut. *Grandpa snoring in the room next to us, and Eddie and I laughing. Mom shushing us, one finger to her lips, and then bursting out in a laugh so loud that Grandpa woke with a snort.*

"Eddie and I slept on cots," I began, but Dad was talking about something else now.

"If only my eyes were better. If only I could have gone."

I moved closer to him, so glad he was there with me and not somewhere in Europe with Eddie.

"We have to keep thinking of places like this," he said. "Things growing, reaching for the sky, instead of being torn down."

It made me think of Grandpa bending over, turning the soil over or patting the plants.

Grandpa.

"What about Grandpa?" I said. "How will he find out about Eddie?"

"Mom asked me to call him long-distance from the post office. I did that, an hour ago."

"What did he say?"

Dad held up his hand. I could see his mouth trembling.

Then he shook his head. "If only he were here with us. Mom would have . . ." He stopped.

If only.

Sometimes, coming home from fishing, late for dinner, Grandpa and I would cross the boulevard, dodging a car or two. I'd hold the tackle box over my arm, the handles making red marks in my skin. Grandpa would slap one hand on top of his head to hold on his cap, and grab my free hand with the other, and we'd run. Mom, seeing us come down the gravel path, would begin to laugh.

Dad was right. He would cheer Mom up in two seconds. He'd tell us how good Eddie was at finding places, tell us about that time when Eddie and I took the wrong path in the Catskills, and Eddie yodeled so someone would find us. Grandpa always laughed about that, too.

Back at the corner I nearly fell over Harlan, who was lying in the street, face to the sun, eyes closed.

What was the matter with him, anyway?

And then I saw Kennis shooting a gun, those two pieces of wood stuck together with a rubber band.

Playing soldiers.

What good was that?

Harlan opened one eye. Orange ice ringed his mouth as if a volcano had just erupted. "I'm a Nazi," he said.

I stepped over him and kept going.

"What about Virginia Tooey?" I asked Dad.

Dad shook his head.

Virginia didn't know, then. She must be in her house, writing letters and knitting khaki socks for Eddie.

As we went up the path I could see Mom, still in her robe, standing by the kitchen window, looking out at us.

She raised one hand, and as we went in the door, she was saying, "This is war. Look at this bare earth in front of us, nothing growing." She held her arms out to Dad. "My child missing."

I stood there for a moment, wishing I were somewhere else. I picked up Judy and buried my face in her warm fur.

Letter for Lily.

Please go in my living room and get Eddie's picture. Send it right away, even if you have to ask your grandmother for the money. Tell her I'll pay her back when the war is over. I can't re-member what Eddie looks like and now he's miss-ing in action, isn't it strange, on a beach. It was on D-day. The telegram didn't come until this morning. He never even got any of the candy.

Margaret

Dear Virginia,

I wanted to tell you that Eddie got lost in France. I know you'd want to know. Eddie thought you were very pretty. He told me that. The prettiest girl he ever saw. He said I might look like you someday.

I hope so.

Listen, I'll let you know when he's found as soon as I can and then you can start writing to him again.

Yours truly,

Meggie Dillon

Dear Grandpa,

Remember the time we were lost in the Catskills and Eddie found the way home?

What do you think, Grandpa? Won't he find his way again?

Love,

Meggie

To the Hot-O Soup Company:

The first thing I'm going to do when the war is over is hope that there won't be another one. And if my brother comes home, I won't need to hope for anything else.

Chapter Thirteen

"Meggie?" Patches said through the wall.

I leaned closer to the wall. "I'm here," I said into the dark.

"Are you okay?"

I wasn't. Everything was wrong. Eddie. Mom and Dad crying. Grandpa alone at home. Owing Arnold the Spy all that money. "If only I hadn't taken the ice cream," I said, then blurted out, "I hate it here."

Patches took a breath. "It's wonderful here," she said slowly. "You can switch the lights on and off, and there's a bathroom inside, and enough money for school shoes."

No electricity, no bathroom. Who ever heard of that? "Where did you come from?"

She didn't answer for a moment. "The mountains," she said.

"When the war is over," I said, "we'll all go home. There'll be parties. . . ."

"That's true," she said. "My three brothers and their wives will come over again on Sundays. My sister, Lou, always brings raisin pies, and Mom will roast a possum."

I covered my mouth. A possum. It sounded worse than Spam.

We were both quiet. I kept thinking about the shoes on Patches' table. And then I fell asleep, to wake up while it was still half dark. I had dreamed of Grandpa and Eddie in the garden, dreamed that I had been left out, watching the two of them talking and laughing. I sat up, tears on my face.

At home in Rockaway I loved to wake up early while everyone else was still asleep. I'd patter around in the kitchen to peer out at the waves, silvery as they folded over on themselves, and listen to the *swish-swish* sounds they made on summer mornings. But this wasn't Rockaway; there was no Atlantic Ocean. Dad was at the factory on the graveyard shift. Only Mom slept; I could hear her mumble as she turned over in her bed.

I went into the rabbit-hutch kitchen. The floor was wet, the linoleum squishing between my toes. Ronnelle must have been doing the wash earlier. Sometimes, if I listened against the wall, I could hear her humming as she put the clothes through the wringer. It was always that pilot song: "Coming In on a Wing and a Prayer." She was thinking about her husband Michael.

I looked out the window. The sky was still dark but the moon was almost full, throwing shadows across the street and onto the kitchen floor. One of Grandpa's sayings was about the moon, but I couldn't remember what it was, only that it had something to do with when to plant, or not to plant.

I swallowed. I went back to my bedroom, standing still on one foot as I heard Mom turn over.

I wondered what Dad was doing at work, what part of a plane he was working on. He said that the motors were made by Rolls-Royce, whoever they were, and that they were the best motors in the world. I wished he were home in the back bedroom, giving me that safe feeling.

Ronnelle was at the factory now, too. Yesterday she had come across the lawn, running, the strings of her Hooverette apron flying, and Lulu toddling along with her. She called as she opened our door, "Mail for me. Michael has only two missions left. Then he's coming—" She broke off, looking at Mom's face. "I'm sorry."

Mom had put her arms around her. "Do you think I'm not happy for you? Oh, Ronnelle."

"But still . . . ," Ronnelle had said. "Two more. I'm so tired of being afraid for him." She leaned her head back to look into Mom's eyes. "If we get through this, I'm going to be the best person."

Mom smiled. "You are that now."

I thought about being the best person, too, and wondered if Eddie felt the same way. I had to smile thinking that sometimes Eddie had gotten himself in trouble. Once on a sunny spring day he had played hooky from school and spent the whole day playing catch with his best friend on 102nd Street. And in fifth grade he had gotten a terrible report card. I still remembered the Cs marching in a row and how angry Mom and Dad had been.

If only I could remember what he looked like. When I concentrated I could picture his eyes and his nose, always a little red from allergies. I knew the feel of his hair, and his hands on mine when he taught me to bat. I just couldn't put it all together into Eddie.

I tiptoed into my bedroom, leaving the door open to the moonlight in the kitchen, and inched out the treasure box. I lifted everything out, my hands gentle on the smashed shells, the postcard collection, easing them onto the floor next to me. And then I ran my hand over the gritty bottom of the box, feeling the seeds still there.

My handkerchief was on the table next to the bed. I dug out the seeds with my fingernails one by one and dropped them into the hanky.

On the way outside, I took a tablespoon from the

kitchen drawer, feeling the dampness on my feet, and then I was in front of the house, the streets empty for once, the SUNDAE, MONDAY, AND ALWAYS truck chained to a tree on the corner.

I knelt down next to the steps, one hand on the stone still warm from yesterday's sun, and began to turn over the earth with the spoon.

It wasn't easy; the soil was packed down, and knobby roots crisscrossed the earth just under the surface. The sound of my breath was in my ears as I crouched there, but as I worked I felt each spoonful of soil turn soft, and as I went deeper, there was moisture that turned and turned with the spoon and I dug my fingers into it the way Grandpa would have, and I couldn't stop seeing his face. "*I haf a garden to grow.*"

Suppose I had thrown my arms around him and said *Come with us to Michigan?*

Would he have come?

But what about the rest of it: "*If this were anywhere else but Rockaway they'd probably put him in jail,*" the boys had said.

Could that be true?

At last I had a patch of earth that could be planted.

I took each seed out of the handkerchief and put it on the earth. "*Things growing,*" Dad had said, "*reaching for the sky.*"

I sprinkled a little of the soil over the top and stood up, almost dizzy from bending over so long.

The stars were fading now; it was almost daytime.

Before I could climb the steps and go into the kitchen, I heard the gritty sound of footsteps in the street: someone coming home from work.

It was Arnold the Spy, and he was walking slowly, coming toward me.

For a moment I wasn't sure if he had seen me. I took a step back, covering the soft earth with one bare heel, my hand to my mouth, hoping that I was wrong, that he'd pass by, going on his way down the street, and never even notice I was there.

I was reminded of a raccoon I had seen once in Grandpa's garden, late, after a party. Everyone was in the kitchen cleaning up, everyone but me.

The raccoon had stopped when he saw me, one delicate paw up in the air, almost frozen against one of Grandpa's plants. I had held on to the porch railing, holding my breath. Then we both had run, the raccoon to go under the fence and me into the house.

Now I clenched my hands together over my mouth and I looked up and saw Arnold's face, and even in the dim early morning light, I knew he had seen me. I knew he was watching me.

He came up the front path toward me. I stood still the

way the raccoon had that night in Rockaway, unable to move. "Why aren't you asleep?" he asked.

I took a step backward. "I was planting seeds."

"By the full moon," he said. "That's a good way to plant."

He sat down on the step, and I sat, too, but on the very edge in case I wanted to run. I wanted to tell him about the key, but I was so afraid, it was hard to open my mouth. After a while I took a breath. "If someone has an accent, would they arrest him here?"

"Of course not. Lots of people have accents," he said. "There are people here from all over."

"Are you sure?"

"This is America, after all," he said.

Then, before I could stop myself, I asked, "How can people really tell if someone's a spy?"

He ran his hand over his hair and sighed. "You can't. But the thing is . . ." He hesitated. "I guess you've got to be careful not to jump to conclusions about people."

I didn't think that was much of an answer, but I didn't know how else to ask. We didn't talk for a while, and I began to think it must be terrible to be a spy . . . without friends, wandering around all night by yourself.

And something else. It was really sad if you had nothing else to do but spy on an eleven-year-old girl who was planting seeds.

I didn't remember what he had said about not jumping to conclusions about people until I was in bed. I fell asleep thinking of those two boys who had painted the swastika on Grandpa's window.

> TO ARNOLD THE ICE CREAM MAN:
>   PLEASE DON'T LEAVE YOUR KEY
> ON TOP OF THE TIRE ANYMORE.
>   HIDE IT.
>   YOURS TRULY,
>   ANONYMOUS

Chapter Fourteen

Mom was gone. Wearing a red snood to cover her hair, and her best polka-dot dress, she'd left for the factory to ask for a job.

"You can stay alone during the day, can't you, Meggie?" she had said. "You're almost grown." She ran her fingers over my hair, straightening my bangs. "And Dad will be sleeping in the bedroom if you need him."

What had Eddie said? *"You'll be the only one home. . . . No more baby."*

"Oh, Meggie." Mom had pulled me to her, hugging me hard, smelling like cold cream and Sweetheart Soap. "I have to do something. I just can't stay home all day and knit socks."

Mouth dry, I had nodded. During the summer at home, I

spent my days wandering around Rockaway, hanging out with Lily, or Grandpa, or by myself, just watching the waves crash onto the beach or throwing bread to the seagulls. I'd slip into the kitchen for a quick cream cheese sandwich with chives when the church bells bonged twelve and slip out again ten minutes later. I never minded being alone.

But that was a different alone, a sunny alone. Even though it was hot today, the sky was gray, and thunder rumbled in the distance.

"Carpe diem," I whispered to Mom, trying to sound as if I didn't mind.

She put her hand on my cheek. "If only I could see Grandpa for two minutes," she said.

Outside, Harlan and Kennis were playing Giant Steps. "Take thirteen banana steps," Harlan said.

Kennis, wearing a pair of shorts that came up almost under his armpits, took thirteen banana steps, twirling back and forth in the street. It took him forever.

Harlan waited until the last minute, watching him, his mouth twisted, trying not to laugh. Then he slapped his leg, snickering. "You forgot to say 'May I?' Start over."

"That's it, Harlan," Kennis yelled, his face beet red. "You think I'm an idiot? I'm not playing with you again for the rest of my life." He stomped off.

Harlan squinted toward our living room window. I was sitting on the foldout couch, smelling the odor of Grandpa's cellar and running my hands over the horrible green plaid. I could imagine what Harlan was thinking. He needed another idiot to play with.

In ten giant steps he was at the window, jumping up to peer inside. The top of his head bobbed up and down two inches away from me. "Hey, Meggie."

I went into the kitchen for something to eat. I pulled out a box of butter cookies, the ones with the hole in the middle, and stuck my finger through one to nibble around the edges.

"What's the matter with you, Meggie? Going to sit inside all day? Is that what they do where you come from?"

I took a couple of cookies for him and opened the door. I didn't look back at it. I knew Mom had put a silver star there instead of the blue one to tell the world Eddie was missing. I swallowed. "I'm not playing Giant Steps."

"Baby game," he said. "I was just trying to be nice to Kennis."

"Sure."

"Where do you come from, anyway?" He yanked up the middle of his shirt and blew on his World's Fair pickle. "It needs shining every once in a while."

I remembered the day Grandpa had gotten me a pickle like that. I was five and . . . "I went to that World's Fair," I told Harlan. "I come from New York, from Rockaway. Every night there are searchlights in the sky looking for enemy planes. We're a big target for the Nazis."

Patches had slid in on the steps next to us.

"Not so exciting," Harlan said, but I hurried on, determined to make him change his mind. "I've seen the Atlantic Ocean a million times," I said. "The waves can be almost as high as a house. And you know that movie? . . ." I stopped for a breath. "The one with King Kong hanging off the Empire State Building? I was right there, too."

Harlan made a face. "You hung off the Empire State Building? I should believe that?"

"No, I *saw* . . ."

He looked bored. "Well, in Detroit . . . ," he began.

Patches leaned forward. "I come from the mountains. And once we had a bear on our front porch."

Harlan and I were silent. Nothing could beat that.

They both leaned forward at the same time, taking cookies from me. Harlan's was gone in three bites. "We have stuff to do," he mumbled, his mouth full.

Patches stood up. "I'm going home for a while. I'm supposed to sweep the walk for my mother."

Harlan and I sat on the steps. Someone across the street had turned on the radio. The Andrews Sisters were singing "Don't Sit Under the Apple Tree."

In the fall, the apples on Grandpa's tree plunked down onto the ground, and one had landed on my head once, leaving a round lump like a small apple itself.

"*We'll put all the apples in the bushel basket,*" Grandpa had said. "*Your mother can make chunky applesauce and maybe a couple of pies.*"

"They're full of worms. Disgusting."

"Not a thing wrong with worms, Margaret. They tunnel through the earth, making it soft so green things will grow."

"Don't call me Margaret, please. If you think I want them tunneling through my stomach . . . Besides, I'm afraid of worms."

He had thrown back his head and laughed. "Oh, Margaret, you have the courage of a lion. But it's all right to be afraid."

"Come on, Meggie, let's go," Harlan said.

"Where?" I asked, but he didn't answer. He started down the street, scooping up a ball. "I declare war on Italy!" he said, bouncing it hard. "I declare war on Germany!"

I followed him, the hazy lemon sun burning a spot in the middle of my head. On a day like this last summer, Grandpa had told me, "I remember the old Germany, Margaret, not hooligans like Hitler who started this war. And when this is over, maybe it will be different. Maybe people will remember and try to be better to each other."

Grandpa's eyes were red and he had said it as if he wasn't sure it would ever happen. "Boats on the river, summer concerts, neighbors." He had walked away from me then, out to the garden, and bent over to touch the feathery leaves of his tomato plants.

Two steps ahead of me, Harlan declared war on the planet Mars. He turned then. "We have to go to the factory."

Chapter Fifteen

"I'm not going to the factory, Harlan. Not in a million years." I could picture Mom right there in front of me. *What are you doing here?*

"Listen," Harlan said. "I know everything that goes on at the factory. Even the guard at the gate. He'll let us in."

"No good," I said. "And why do we want to go there, anyway?"

"It's about your brother. I know he might be dead."

I felt a terrible burst of anger, and then fear, such fear that I almost couldn't swallow.

I looked up at the sun. If you stared at it long enough, you'd be blind in ten years or so. I took a breath. "Don't say that, Harlan! My brother isn't . . ."

"I didn't mean it that way," Harlan said. "I meant I was going to help find him."

What was he talking about? "How?" I had trouble saying that one word.

"I told you. I know the guard at the gate. I even brought him ice cream the other day."

Another scratch mark on the fender.

Harlan didn't wait for me. "There's someone we have to see," he said over his shoulder. "His name is Terry. He works in the wings."

And then we were there, at the factory with women in kerchiefs like Rosie the Riveter, men in overalls with black lunch pails, some of them sitting on the edge of the wall with their eyes closed as if they were napping.

What did Eddie have to do with this factory? Eddie, who hadn't known what a B-24 was when he went into the army.

"We're leaving soon," Harlan said. "Going back to Detroit before school starts."

I could hear Dad's voice that first day. *They come and they go.* I stared at him. "You're going home?"

"That's what I said." He was grinning. "Couple of weeks." He swiped his arm across his face.

I opened my mouth. Harlan wasn't really my friend. I hardly knew him, hardly knew Kennis or their mother, who had said *"Ah"* on the other side of the wall. But it was just too much.

Harlan squinted up at the sun. He was going to be blind,

too. "My mom and dad made money building planes," he said. "They're going to take that money now. My dad is going into the army. Going to fight in the Pacific, I guess. He wants to be a hero like Uncle Leo."

My mouth was dry. Lily's father was fighting in the war, and she hated it.

Harlan seemed to know what I was thinking. "I don't worry about my father. He's the toughest guy I know."

A man sat at a table in front of the factory gate, watching as groups of people came in and others left. All of them had tags like Dad's pinned to their shirts.

The guard didn't seem to be worried about the top-secret factory. His feet were up on the edge of the table. He had a huge hole in the sole of his left shoe.

"All right if we go inside?" Harlan asked him. "We have to see someone."

The guard stared at us; he barely lifted a thumb to motion us past him and onto the cement walk just beyond. I held back, thinking of Mom, but Harlan waved furiously, so I went after him.

Inside was an open space, bustling with people who moved things on huge carts that sped past us. Over our heads were slabs of metal plane parts, and there was an odd smell of glue or paint in the air.

I didn't have to worry about Mom's seeing me. So many people wandered around, drilling, scraping, yelling—hundreds of them—that if it had been the other way around and

I had been searching, really wanting to find her, I'd never have been able to do it.

"Hey, kids," someone yelled. "What are you doing?"

Harlan never stopped. He dodged the man who was calling us and skittered down an aisle, jumping over a pile of tools that was in his way.

I ran, too, pretending I was invisible, passing women who were riveting plane parts together.

Harlan cupped his hands around his mouth: "Terry? Where the heck are you?" And then he stopped and pointed. I couldn't believe what I was seeing. Someone was inside the wing of the plane, someone smaller than I was.

The man grinned at us and popped out of the wing, hanging there until his feet found the ladder. He jumped off the last rung and wiped his hands on a cloth that hung out of his pocket.

"Terry"—Harlan waved his hand—"this is Meggie. Her brother's missing in action. Probably—"

"Don't say that."

The man looked up at me, his head turned to one side.

He reached out with one hand and put it on my shoulder. "Missing," he said. "Not dead. No."

I nodded, narrowing my eyes at Harlan. *See? You don't know everything*, I wanted to say.

But the man, Terry, motioned to us to follow him around the side of the wing to sink down against the wall. It was cool there against the cement.

"We're going home at the end of the summer," Harlan told Terry.

"Ah," Terry said.

"*Ah.*" Like Harlan's mother, Mrs. Tucker.

If I were the one leaving, I'd say, *Going back to Rockaway, going back to my bedroom where the ceiling shimmers from the water, back to digging in Grandpa's garden.* I swallowed. *Back to Grandpa.*

Terry rubbed his knees and his legs, which poked out in front of him. "Lucky. So lucky."

"I know it," Harlan said. Were there tears in his eyes? Could that be? He was as homesick as Kennis, then. As homesick as I was.

And then I saw there were tears in Terry's eyes, too.

"Why don't you go back?" I blurted out. If I had been grown and could do what I wanted, I would have left that minute.

Terry opened his eyes, blue and clear. "In Germany, Hitler is killing anyone who's different. . . . Different religions, old people, sick people." He squinted up at the wing of the plane. "Little people like me."

He leaned forward. "We have to do what we think is right, no matter how hard it is." He smiled then. "I'm doing my bit. Not many can get into the spaces inside the plane that I can. And when it's over . . . ah, when it's over, I'm going back to the mountains to sit on my porch and rock forever. Knowing that keeps me going."

I put my head back against that cool wall, watching everything that went on. A great wing, attached to runners on the ceiling, rode high over my head, going from one part of the factory to another.

If only I could squeeze into one of those wings the way Terry did, fly to Normandy, France, and look for Eddie myself.

"This is what you want to do." Harlan pulled a piece of paper out of his pocket and folded it into a piece so small you could hardly see it.

Terry looked from Harlan to me. "You want to send a message to the pilot?" For a moment I thought he looked sad; then he stood up, leaning against the ladder. I wondered if I had imagined it.

Harlan nodded. "Write what your brother looks like. Say he's probably wandering around somewhere." He snapped his fingers. "Maybe he has that thing when you get hit on the head. You know, you can't remember anything, not even your name."

I closed my eyes. Strange. Harlan thought the way I did after all. Eddie wasn't really missing. He was just lost. But then suddenly a thought came into my mind, and I knew it had been there all along. Being missing wasn't the same as being lost.

Don't think that, I told myself, but I knew it was true.

"Don't you see," Harlan said. "This pilot might go to France, right? He'll talk to people. And maybe . . ."

I thought of all the notes in the bottles we had dropped into the surf in Rockaway with our names and addresses. We had never seen them again, had never heard from one person. Writing to a pilot was just like that.

I couldn't look at Terry. Still, I took the paper, trying to think of what I could write to a pilot I didn't know.

In the end, I didn't write about Eddie at all. Instead, I wrote that I would be thinking about that pilot, hoping he was safe. But it was Eddie I thought about as I wrote: the way his teeth were separated, that he could yodel, and that he dated a girl named Virginia Tooey. I thought, too, that sometimes I was angry because Eddie was Grandpa's favorite when I wanted to be. And I remembered he had said, "*Going to win the war for you, Meg.*"

If only I could remember what he looked like.

Someday my note would be in France, high in the sky, somewhere over Eddie's head even though he didn't know it. I added a line on the bottom so small that no one could really read it: *Come home, Eddie. You can be Grandpa's favorite.*

Terry was watching me; it was almost as if he knew what I was thinking.

"Never mind," he said. "Men are wandering all over Europe." He waved his hand. "When it's over, we'll all go back home." Home. Harlan and I went back out of the factory, Harlan marching ahead of me as if he owned the place, and outside he stopped to wave at the guard, almost like a salute.

Chapter Sixteen

"Hey." I peeked through the hole. Patches was clomping around in her school shoes.

She slid over to peer in at me. "Trying to get used to them. They're not as comfortable as I thought they'd be. I can feel them rubbing against my heels."

"There's nothing to do," I said.

"How about . . . ," she began, and stamped away from the wall. I could see her mother's feet in the doorway.

"You'll have those shoes worn out," she told Patches. "How about helping me with the dishes."

I wandered outside. Mom and Dad were sitting on the step in front of the house. It was Mom's day off, and Dad had come out of the bedroom. "Hard to sleep in the daylight," he said, yawning.

"Strange living like this," Mom said. "Sometimes when I'm drilling holes in huge pieces of metal, one after another in a row, the noise of it coming through my earplugs, my head in a kerchief, my eyes in those goggles, I can't believe it's me. I think I'm going to wake up at home, knitting on the couch or cooking supper in the kitchen . . . and then I think of Eddie." She put one of her arms around me. "I miss you while I'm working."

I leaned against her. Mom always smelled good, a little like starch, a little like perfume. "You feel like a plump pigeon," I told her, reminding her of the bird game Eddie and I used to play.

She smiled a little. "What about Ronnelle? What is she?"

I thought for a moment. "I think a wren," I said. "You know, they're speckled, and sweet."

Ronnelle had a book in her hand as she sat on her steps and watched Lulu play with a Tinkertoy in her stroller. She waved the book. "Studying science."

Worse than geography.

"We're going to take turns, Michael and I. Both of us want to become teachers after the war."

Everyone was quiet then, Ronnelle turning pages, Mom's head back against the screen door, her eyes puffy. She'd been crying again, I knew that, even though she tried to hide it from me.

I'd tell Hot-O Soup that what I really wanted was to make my mother happy again.

"Harlan said Arnold the ice cream man is a spy," I said.

Dad shook his head. "Where did he get that idea?"

"Arnold's not in the army."

"Good," Mom said almost under her breath. "If he isn't in the army, he's safe."

Who could worry about Arnold's being safe? He was tall, much taller than Eddie, and strong.

Dad reached out and circled Mom's wrist with his fingers. "Even so, I'm proud of Eddie. You are, too."

Mom made a sound in her throat.

"Lots of reasons why people aren't in the army," Dad said. "Maybe he's not old enough."

"He is. He had a birthday weeks ago. Harlan said that, too. Someone told him."

I thought about it. Arnold didn't look like someone who had a birthday. I couldn't picture him when he was young, wearing a party hat, blowing a paper horn, cutting the first slice of cake with his mother's hand on his.

Next door, Harlan and Kennis were fighting. There was the sound of glass breaking. "No wonder we have wars," I heard Harlan's mother begin. "You two can't even . . ." Her voice trailed off.

"That Harlan." Dad shook his head. "Don't pay attention to what he says."

I saw Dad stiffen then, and heard the sound of the truck. Not Arnold's truck. This was a mail truck, special delivery.

Mom sat up straight; her hand went to her throat, leaving marks across her skin.

The brown jeep drove up the street slowly, and Mrs. Tucker came out on her step. I heard Ronnelle close her book with a little snap.

Everything was still. The jeep passed house after house. A telegram for someone, I thought. Someone missing? Someone killed in action?

He stopped in front of our door, and I wanted to stand up, but I couldn't move. Then Dad was up off the step and walking down to meet him halfway.

At last I saw it wasn't a telegram. The mailman came up the path holding out a small package so we all could see it.

For a moment Dad stood there with the mailman; then he turned back to us. "It's for Meggie," he told Mom. "From your father. That's all, just for Meggie."

Next to me, Mom began to sob.

"It's all right," I said, touching her arm. "All right."

Dad handed the package to me and raised Mom up off the step. "My dear Ingrid," he said. He opened the door and they went inside.

I held the package in my hands, ran my fingers over it,

and then I heard Mom turning on the faucet to fill a glass of water. "I am proud of him," she said, her voice thick. "It's just so hard."

There was the rumble of Dad's voice. "Remember when we went to the Catskills? I was so worried about spending that money. I'm so glad we did. So glad . . ."

I glanced across at Ronnelle. Her head was down on the book in her lap. She looked up at me, the color gone from her cheeks. "Oh, Meggie, I thought it was Michael." Her mouth was open as if she was having trouble breathing.

I looked down at the package, postmarked the day after we had heard Eddie was missing, a small box wrapped over and over with a Bohack's store brown bag and garden string, addressed to me, *Miss Margaret Dillon,* in Grandpa's square letters.

I brought it inside to the kitchen. Mom and Dad were sitting at the table, holding hands across the scarred wood.

"I'm trying to coo like a pigeon," Mom said with a watery smile, and I bent over her with the box in my hand to give her a kiss. Then I sat between them and unwrapped the package.

Inside, wrapped in waxed paper, was Grandpa's Victory medal from the Great War. I looked down at it, hardly believing he had sent it. I ran my fingers over it, gently touching the angel's outspread wings, her flowing skirt, the sword in her hand. I patted the ribbon with its faded rainbow stripes, reminding myself of Grandpa patting the leaves of his cucumber plants the day we had left for Willow Run.

Why hadn't he given it to Eddie? I wondered, thinking of the day Eddie had left. *Eddie hugging us all, hugging Grandpa last, Grandpa's arms wrapped around him, tears in his eyes. "Edvard."*

Not to Eddie. Eddie, his favorite. Eddie, everyone's favorite.

Me. He had given it to me.

Mom looked up, her mouth open in a round O. "I wonder why he sent it." Then: "He always cherished that medal, Meggie."

"I wish he were here." I'd have given anything to put my head out the door and see him walking up the street, even with that red hat, even with an *Apfelstrudel* in his hands and even with his accent.

Mom leaned over and fished a piece of loose-leaf out of the bottom of the box. "Read it, Meggie," she said.

I began to read aloud, and then I couldn't get the words out, so I finished it to myself and slid it gently across the table so they could see it:

Liebe *Margaret,*

   My cucumbers are grown. Yesterday I brought in a bushel basket of them to make into pickles. The sun was shining on the back window and it made me think of brining the pickles last year with you and Edward. Such a happy memory. And do you know what the shine on the window showed me, Margaret? The outline was so faint I might never have seen it. I would never have known what you did for me that night. What was it you called it when we saw the mark on your sleeve? Victory Red.

So I send you my Victory medal because what you did was brave. I send it to you so you will be brave when you need to be brave. And I send it to you because there is no one I love more.

Grandpa

We sat there without talking for a moment; then Mom asked, "But what did you do?"

I was crying now, so I didn't have to talk. I didn't have to tell them.

Mom shook her head. "They always had secrets, my father and Meggie. How lovely for them both."

Dear Grandpa,

I'm sorry you found out about the paint.

The medal is the best thing anyone ever gave me in my life. I will keep it forever. I'll never lose it.

I love you.

Meggie

Chapter Seventeen

I went to bed with the medal on my pillow, thinking that school would start in a few days, and that Harlan was going back to Detroit tomorrow. But most of all I thought of Grandpa.

I could hear Patches turn over on the other side of the wall and I leaned over to tap: *bing bing bing bong.*

"Want a Necco Wafer?" she asked. "I can't see in the dark, but the ones that are left are probably pink."

There was just enough room to slide one through. Mom would have a fit; I had already brushed my teeth.

"Pink?" Patches asked as I chewed.

"Mmm, the worst kind." I took a breath, and then I was telling her about Grandpa, telling her that he had come from Germany instead of Mongolia, telling her about the swastika and that some people thought he was a spy.

I was hoping she'd say that of course he wasn't a spy, that anyone who had a Victory medal was a hero. But she didn't say anything like that.

I could hear her voice now, close to the opening in the wall. "You think I'm so tough."

What was that all about? I shook my head, thinking of Patches with her ten stitches, Patches jumping rope, her bare feet pounding on the street among the bits of dirt and stones. *Tough as nails*, Grandpa would say.

What she said next was so low, so hesitant, that I wasn't sure I had heard it right. "Say that again?"

"I never had a pair of shoes before. We never had the money."

But everyone had shoes! There were always piles of them on the boardwalk when we went swimming. Sometimes I even came home with someone else's. Shoes thrown in the closet. Wearing my mother's high-heel shoes. How could you not have shoes, even though leather was rationed? "But what about school?" I asked slowly. "And church?"

"We never had the money until now," she said. "Most of the kids I knew didn't have shoes, either."

I remembered seeing her marching around in those shoes in her bedroom. Her first shoes!

I poked my finger through the hole in the wall, and a moment later, she gave it a tap.

It was hard to keep my eyes open, but just before I fell asleep, I heard her whisper, "I screamed so loud when I had stitches that some kid told me I was a big baby."

And then, when it seemed as if I had just shut my eyes, it was morning. Harlan was going home today. Lucky Harlan.

I threw on my clothes, grabbed a piece of paper and a pencil, and rushed outside.

Kennis sat in the back of the Tuckers' car, but all I could see was the top of his head and one hand. His fingers tapped on the pile of boxes next to him as if he were plinking on a piano. I wondered where Harlan was.

Mr. Tucker came down the path with still more boxes in his arms, and in the doorway, Mrs. Tucker shook the mop until feathery balls of dust flew through the air and landed on the cement.

She smiled at me, blowing at a strand of pale hair on her forehead. "Have to leave the place better than I found it. A lot better."

I thought about thanking her for saying "Ah" that night, but I didn't even want to think about it. Instead, I raised my hand to wave.

Harlan dashed out the door, bumping into his mother and the mop. He skidded off the step, then righted himself. In the car, Kennis began to laugh.

I waved the paper at Harlan. "I want to get your address," I said as he crossed the little square of beaten-down grass to sit on my stoop. "I like to write letters."

He twitched one shoulder. "I'm not much on writing myself."

"Still," I said.

"I guess." He reached for the paper and scribbled down an address I could hardly read. "You probably won't write anyway," he said.

"I will, really." Then, before I could stop myself, I said, "You look different. You look . . ." I bit my lip. I didn't want to say *cleaner*. He did look cleaner, though, his hair slicked back with water, his shirt with only one or two spots, the World's Fair pickle gleaming.

"Going home," he said. "What do you think? I have to look good to see everybody." He squinted toward the car. "There's something I have to talk to you about before I never see you again."

"Don't say that."

"You live . . . where? Rockaway? I never even heard of that place before you came," he said. "I've never been to New York. Never seen the ocean."

I didn't know exactly where Detroit was, either.

"When I'm grown up," I began, then raised one shoulder the way he had. He was right. I'd never get to Detroit and he'd never get to New York. Wasn't that strange? In a few minutes he'd be gone forever, and even though I'd known him only a couple of weeks, he'd be there in my head until I was at least as old as Grandpa.

I stared at him so I'd remember his face, the light eyes, the few freckles, his ears flat to his head. I wished I had done that with Eddie, stared at him hard enough to remember him forever.

"We owe Arnold the Spy a lot of money," Harlan said. "More than I can count."

"I know I have to pay him back," I said. "I have this week's allowance, and I can ask Dad for next week's. . . ." I thought for a moment. "And the week after that, maybe."

Dad would wonder why.

And how was I going to get the money to Arnold? Suppose I left it on the seat of the truck? I saw myself climbing up on the running board, looking over my shoulder to see his angry face a step in back of me. It was like a terrible movie I had seen with Grandpa one time. *"Watch out, he's got a gun! More popcorn, Margaret?"*

But Grandpa wasn't here to make it seem less scary. He was home, weeding his garden. I glanced down over the step, but his seeds weren't growing. Maybe they'd all washed out in the rain the other day.

I leaned over farther. I knew that spot by heart, the five stones I had laid against the wall of the house so they'd be out of the way, the faint ridges in the earth where I had planted the seeds. *Grow,* I told them, *grow.*

At the curb Mr. Tucker opened the front door of the

car. "Let's go, Harley," he called. "Got a long way to drive before dark."

Mrs. Tucker locked the apartment and dropped the key back into the mail slot in the door. She leaned her head against the wall for just an instant, then came down the path. "I'll never forget this place," she said. "It was a hard time, a terrible time." She bit her lip. "Tell your mom and dad I'm praying for them, and praying for your brother."

I crossed the lawn and she hugged me there on the front path. "I hope you'll go home soon, Meggie." She touched my shoulder, shaking her head. "This war has done something to every single one of us."

"Harlan!" Mr. Tucker called again.

"I'm coming, aren't I?" Harlan said, but he didn't get up from my stoop.

I hesitated, then went back to him.

"Listen, Meggie," he said. "I've got to go. Just give this to Arnold the Spy." He reached into his pocket and pulled out a dollar bill.

I had seen it before, creased and old: his uncle Leo's hardware-store dollar.

"Tell him it's the best thing I ever had." Harlan's eyes filled as he looked down at it. He unfolded it. "Look. My uncle's initials in pencil. *L.T.* I did that so they'd always be there."

I put my hands behind my back. "Don't do it, Harlan." I could hardly talk.

Mr. Tucker tapped the horn now, a short, warning sound, and Harlan grabbed my elbow. "I thought I had a year to pay him back, even two years. But there's no time left." He opened my curled fingers and put the dollar bill in my hand. "Tell him my uncle was a hero. Leo Tucker."

I watched him zigzag across the grass, calling back over his shoulder. "Tell him to take good care of it," he called. "It's all I have left of my uncle."

"I will." I took a step after him, wondering how I would ever do that.

Harlan slid into the car, giving Kennis a little punch. "You have to take up all the room?" He rolled down the window and stuck out his head. "If Eddie doesn't come back, maybe you'll get some money from the government, enough to buy a hardware store of your own."

"Harlan!" I heard Mrs. Tucker say.

"You could come to Detroit," he yelled, his voice almost lost beneath the sound of the motor as Mr. Tucker pulled away. "We could be partners."

"He's coming back," I yelled, my voice loud in my ears. "Don't you worry about that."

The apartment door opened on the other side of me. "Good luck," Ronnelle called, and Lulu waved both hands.

And Patches came running. "Good luck, Harlan."

And there was Mom out on the step, ready for work, going across the lawn to say goodbye.

The Tuckers drove down the street then, the motor not catching right somehow, the muffler banging as they turned the corner.

I went back inside and sat on the foldout couch in the living room, tightening my fist around Harlan's dollar bill.

Chapter Eighteen

It was almost time for Mom to go to work. She rushed around hanging socks and underwear on a line across the kitchen. "Oh, Meggie," she said. "Last year this time we were in Rockaway sweeping the sand off the front steps." Her mouth quivered. "I'd be putting on a second cup of coffee for Grandpa. How I miss him."

She arched her back. "Can you imagine, I spend my days helping to put huge bombers together . . . almost like sewing up a skirt on the machine at home."

I thought of Terry, Harlan's friend, the man who was shorter than I was, working inside the wings.

After Mom left I could see a puddle of soapy water in front of the washing machine, and drips across the floor from the laundry. The wringer was hardly working, but Dad had said it was just for the duration anyway.

The duration again.

I found the mop and swished it back and forth, making shiny arcs across the red linoleum. The sun slanted through the window onto the floor, drying it quickly; the clock tick-clicked up over the stove, and it almost seemed that the faucet dripped out Arnold's name.

I went into my room and sat on the edge of the bed, the springs creaking. I must have awakened Dad in the other bedroom. "Are you all right in there, Meggie?" he called, his voice thick with sleep.

"Sure," I managed to get out. I ran my fingers over the bedspread. Judy or Jiggs had chewed on the little balls of chenille and I could see the sheet underneath. Harlan's dollar was there, under the pillow.

I had to give it to Arnold, give him my allowance, and tell him . . .

Tell a spy.

I slid out the dollar and patted my pocket to be sure I had Grandpa's medal in there for courage; then I tiptoed out so I wouldn't wake Dad. It was time to find the SUNDAE, MONDAY, AND ALWAYS truck.

The truck wasn't on our block or the next. I was about to give up when I saw it ahead of me, slowly turning the corner.

By the time I reached the end of the street, Arnold the Spy was chaining the truck to a tree halfway down the block.

I could have called out; I could have run after him. I didn't, though. I stood there thinking about the scratches on the running board and what he was going to say.

He put the key underneath the back fender. For a spy he certainly wasn't very smart. I followed him as he walked away, wondering where he was going.

He crossed the street, and halfway down I crossed after him. He went a long way and I kept myself almost a whole block in back of him. And then the streets came to an end, and there was the field Dad had shown me, and I could see Arnold was going to that house across the field, and if I didn't call him it would be too late. He'd be inside with the door closed and I'd never have the courage to knock.

"Arnold," I called, my voice with that rusty sound again.

He stopped ahead of me and turned.

I walked toward him slowly, taking baby steps, until I couldn't make myself go any closer. "Do you know Harlan Tucker?" I couldn't look at his face; I stared down at the Queen Anne's lace and buttercups in the field in front of me.

He raised one shoulder. "Dirty-looking kid? The one who wears the World's Fair pickle?"

"That's what I want to talk to you about." I reached into my pocket, feeling the grosgrain ribbon and Grandpa's medal under my fingers. I held it tight.

"A World's Fair pickle?" He took a few steps closer to me, and I wondered if I should run, so I put up one hand, almost like a policeman, and he stopped.

"Something else," I said. "And something about me, too."

Someone was calling him from the house. I looked up. "You have a mother?"

He glanced over his shoulder and waved. "Of course I have a mother."

"We took your ice cream," I said. "Lots of ice cream."

And then all of it was spilling out, words tumbling one over another: my allowance, and Uncle Leo's dollar bill, the only thing Harlan had left of him.

"You wrote the note about the key," he said.

I nodded.

"I thought so. You were always writing things. . . ."

"You watched. . . ."

"I see everything," he said.

I looked up at him, surprised to see that his face had re-arranged itself. It was round, and acne marks dotted his cheeks. He didn't look angry or even like a spy.

And then I realized I had said it aloud, gasped it aloud through my crying. "You don't look like a spy."

"Spies don't look like spies," he said. "They look like ordinary people."

But then he took a step backward, and I could see the red come into his face. "I'm not a spy." He raised his hand to his mouth, and his fingers weren't quite steady. "But I'm a coward."

Chapter Nineteen

I turned the corner to see Dad standing on the front step. "Meggie," he called, and I went toward him, still thinking of Arnold. Arnold with tears spilling down over those acne marks on his cheeks.

I had wanted to run away from him, but I hadn't. The whole time we talked I had kept one hand in my pocket, clutching Grandpa's medal so hard it made dented crescents in my palm.

"Where have you been?" Dad said now. "Mom is home, we're both waiting." He pushed up his glasses so he looked like an owl. "And you have mail again, Meggie."

I looked up at him quickly, but he shook his head. Not Eddie, then.

Mom was in the kitchen. The wash on the line was dry now, and she was sorting socks, dark ones for Dad, stripes and plain for me. And on the table was a letter in a pale blue envelope and a package addressed to me.

"Like Christmas." Mom rolled the socks into balls and piled them into neat mounds on the table.

I didn't know which to open first, so I slit open the blue envelope with neat slanted handwriting and circles instead of dots over the *i*'s. "It's from Virginia Tooey."

Mom glanced at Dad. "I never thought of Virginia," she said. "I should have written. If only I had thought . . ." She broke off and went to the counter to begin a Spam loaf. "Poor Virginia. What did she say?"

I opened the letter: *"Dear Meggie, I'm so glad you wrote to me. I know about Eddie. All of Rockaway does, every single one praying for him. But I want to tell you something, Meggie. I know he's coming home. Just believe it. He promised me. Love, Virginia."*

For a moment there was silence. Then Mom turned from the sink. "It's the first time," she said, "the first one who has given me hope." She raised both hands almost the way the choir in church did on Sundays. *"All of Rockaway praying."*

Have hope. That's what Grandpa would say. *Haf hope.*

Mom came to the table. She leaned over to take the letter from me and held it up to her face. "I believe it," she said.

"I have to believe it." She put her arms around me. "And you, Meggie, writing to her. How grown-up you've become this summer."

I sat there with Dad across the table, nodding at me and smiling a little. He reached out to reread the letter as Mom went back to the counter. He cleared his throat. "I like Virginia Tooey, I really do."

We listened to Mom stirring the wooden mixing spoon against the bowl. She began to hum the pilot song Ronnelle was always singing: "Coming In on a Wing and a Prayer." It was the first time I had heard her sing since the soldiers had come to tell us Eddie was missing.

I reached for the package next. I knew what it was even before I saw Lily's large handwriting on the front. I un-wrapped it slowly, telling Mom and Dad that I had asked for Eddie's picture, and when the last piece of paper fell away, there was his face.

As I looked at it, it was as if something happened inside my head; things rearranged themselves the way they had with Arnold; the look of Eddie slid together in my mind like a puzzle I had just finished. I could see him so clearly it was as if he were standing right there in front of me.

Not the Eddie in the picture, who was a little fuzzy, but Eddie himself now, Eddie yodeling, dancing down the front step, Eddie swinging me around once on my birthday.

I closed my eyes so I'd never forget again.

Mom came back to the table, wiping her hands on her apron. "He's coming home someday," she said.

Dad reached out and covered my hand. "Good, Meggie, so good that you asked for the picture." He propped it up against the napkin holder on the table and stared at it, nodding. "With Eddie smiling at us here, it almost seems as if we're a family again."

"If only . . ." Mom broke off and went back to the counter.

I knew she was thinking the same thing I was. I rolled up the string and folded the wrapping paper into a square. If only Grandpa were there in the kitchen to feel the way we did, that Eddie would come home someday.

When everything was cleared away, I realized there was another envelope underneath, an official-looking letter with its row of stamps and the bold black return address: *Hot-O Soup Company, Battle Creek, Michigan.*

Mom and Dad watched me. "We hid it underneath for you, Meggie," Dad said. "It could be a great surprise."

"I wonder . . ." My heart began to thump. I tore it open and began to read: *"Dear Miss Dillon, You have won an honorable mention in our soup contest. We are delighted to send you this certificate and five dollars. Your entry warmed our hearts as our soup does for the soldiers, sailors, and marines who are fighting for us overseas."*

I had won something at last.

"Oh, Meggie," Mom said. "Won't Grandpa be happy when he hears about this?"

All those contests Grandpa and I had entered. We were going to see the sights in New York City with our first winnings, and now he wasn't even here.

"What did you say to win this?" Dad asked.

I blinked. "I don't know. I wrote so many. . . ."

In celebration, Mom opened a jar of the strawberry jam that hadn't broken the first day. We slathered it on toast and ate it with the Spam loaf, looking at Eddie's picture with my brand-new five-dollar bill propped up in front of it.

And then we realized how late it was: time for Dad to go to work, and for Mom and me to go to bed. I wondered if Harlan had gotten home yet. I wondered where Eddie was.

I knelt on the floor in my bedroom, reaching under the mattress to feel Eddie's envelope, and pulled it out.

I held it up to my face the way Mom had held Virginia Tooey's letter, but I didn't open it. *Just believe it. He's coming home.* And then I put it back under the mattress.

I lay in bed and tapped on the wall to talk to Patches. She was half asleep, but I told her about Harlan with the dollar bill. I didn't tell her about the rest of it, though. It was all too much to think about.

"Harlan wasn't such a bad kid after all," she said, and her voice trailed off.

I was still wide awake and remembered Grandpa's seeds

and the little salad garden I had planted outdoors. It wasn't as dark in the bedroom tonight as most nights. The kitchen window reflected a piece of the moon so it spilled out onto the linoleum floor. Just this morning, I told myself, none of the seeds had begun to grow. Not one. But somehow tonight might be different. *Have to have hope.*

I pulled on my Snow White bathrobe and tiptoed through the kitchen, taking the flashlight off the counter-top. I opened the door and the two cats followed me outside to sit with me on the stoop, cool after the hot summer day.

I didn't have to worry about Arnold the Spy coming after me. I knew now that he couldn't sleep, that he wandered around the streets of Willow Run every night trying to think of what to do.

I didn't let myself look at the little patch of earth right away; instead, I listened to someone playing the Victrola in one of the apartments across the street. It was that song that had followed us across the country: *"We'll meet again."*

I shined the flashlight over the side of the step. There weren't any shoots yet, but I thought of what Grandpa would say. *Haf to have hope.*

"I do," I told the little patch of dirt. "I have hope for Eddie."

> *Dear Harlan,*
>   *I told you I would write. Here is your uncle Leo's dollar bill.*

Arnold said to tell you that he couldn't take it.

He said he knows you feel sorry about the ice cream and that's enough for him.

I found out about Arnold. He's not a spy, but I can't tell you the rest.

Your friend,

Meggie

Chapter Twenty

The days were cooler now, the sky that brilliant blue just before fall comes; August was over and we were into September. The Allied soldiers had swept their way across France and were heading into Germany, and it was the Wednesday after Labor Day, the first day of school.

Patches was outside ahead of me, wearing her shoes, twirling around. My shoes were the scratched ones from the spring, but I didn't care. Dad had shined most of the marks away, and Ronnelle had made matching plaid hair bows for Patches and me.

On the way to school, I met Terry from the factory, and he grinned up at me, saying that one of these days the factory was going to shut down. "The war in Europe will end by next spring, and the last plane will come along the assembly line soon," he said. "Every one of us will sign our names on the nose cone so the plane will carry us overseas. Even Henry Ford." He put his hand on my shoulder. "The way you did with your letter."

I waved to him over my shoulder. *Home by next spring.*

I spent the day in school, third seat, third row, next to Patches, and it wasn't one bit different from my school in Rockaway, except that now I looked at everyone's shoes, wondering how many kids were wearing them for the first time.

Just before dismissal Mrs. Roe scraped the chalk across the blackboard, writing in large white letters. I watched the two words appear, *carpe diem,* and was so surprised I didn't even raise my hand when she asked if any of us knew what it meant. Next to me, Patches called out, "Seize the day," and smiled at me. I had told her about Grandpa and his sayings. I thought back to the letter I had written the day I had talked to Arnold. *Carpe diem.*

"Yes," Mrs. Roe said. "That's what we'll do this year. Take the initiative, learn what we have to . . ."

A speech I'd heard every year since I began school.

I reached into my pocket and touched Grandpa's medal. I held it as we lined up to march out of school, and instead of going home, I said, "See you in a little while," to Patches, and went to look for Arnold, remembering that day he had said he was a coward:

"I have my draft notice," he said, his eyes filling. "I've had it for almost the whole summer."

"I don't understand."

"My birthday was in June. I was supposed to go into the service. . . ."

Eddie, eighteen. My mother: "What have you done?"

"I have a garden out back," Arnold said. "My mother can't care for it alone. What will happen to the vegetables, the fruit . . ." He stopped. "That's not really it. I'm afraid to go."

"Afraid," I said like an echo.

"I see terrible things at the movies. People killing each other. Blowing each other up. Men being captured and held in terrible prison camps."

I put the dollar bill, still folded, into Arnold's hand. "That's from Harlan. He knows it isn't enough, not nearly enough, but he'll send you more someday."

Arnold looked down at the money. "I'm the last one to drive the ice cream truck. We've been passing it down. First my brother Stan. He's in the Pacific now. Then Charlie, on a ship somewhere."

I handed him a little pile of money, dimes and nickels. "This is for the ice cream I took. I still owe you two dimes, but don't worry, as soon as I get my allowance . . ." I broke off. "I'm never going to steal anything again. It's not worth it." I looked across the field at the daisies. "It gives the ice cream a strange taste."

"That's what being a coward does," he said. "It changes the taste of everything."

And now, after that first day of school, with the blue sky overhead, I was on my way to find him, to tell him part of the letter I had just received from Grandpa.

I looked everywhere, and was about to give up when I saw the SUNDAE, MONDAY, AND ALWAYS truck parked across the street from the movie theater. I waited until he came outside, blinking in the daylight.

He saw me at the same time. "I've been looking for you for the last few days," he said. "Want an ice cream?"

I shook my head, watching two kids come down the street. I waited until he had handed them sundaes and they were halfway down the block again. Then I pulled out the medal to show him. "It was my grandfather's," I said.

He took it in his hand, holding it up. "He must be a great guy," he said.

I nodded, and then I said something I never thought I'd say. "He was born in Germany. You can tell because he has an accent." I rushed on. "At home in Rockaway, boys covered his window with a swastika just because of it."

"Terrible." Arnold shook his head. "I've been thinking about it. Everyone around me is doing the best he can: Harlan with the dollar bill, my brothers. You know, there's even a guy who's only about three feet tall. He spends his days in the tiniest spaces building planes." He shuddered. "I don't know how he can do that, squeezed in . . ." He wiped his eyes. "Everyone's doing something but me."

He looked down the street, his lips pressed together; then he nodded. "You're right. I have to go."

I raised my shoulders in the air. "I didn't say that."

We both smiled; then I took a breath. "The medal is for you to take with you. I wrote to my grandfather . . ."

He shook his head. "I can't."

"Really you can. We would be glad. My grandpa and I."

I thought of Grandpa the day I had said goodbye to him, Grandpa touching the medal. "Grandpa said he was afraid. And once, he said it was all right for me to be afraid."

Arnold was smiling just a bit. "And will the medal keep me safe?"

"I . . . I don't think so," I said carefully. "But it would be good to have anyway, something to hold on to." And in back of my mind: *Haf to have hope.*

He nodded. "I don't even know your name."

"Margaret," I said. "I'm named for my grandmother."

He reached into the freezer and brought out an ice cream bag. "Put down your New York address. I'll send it back to you when the war is over. I'll never forget."

As I took the paper I could see his hands were trembling; he was still afraid. I would be afraid, too. I scribbled my address on the bag. "It's just a loan," I said. "I'll need it back."

"I promise."

"Then you'll have to be all right," I said.

"That's what I was thinking." He put his hand on top of my head. "My luck has changed. Ever since the first day you came and made a face at me."

I touched the medal once more. And then from up the street I heard Ronnelle calling my name, calling and waving her hand.

I turned to go, but Arnold called after me. "When this is over, I'm going to spend my days making sure wars like this never happen again."

"How?"

"That's what we all have to figure out," he said. "Every one of us."

Now Lulu was calling. "Hurry, Honey. Hurry."

And Ronnelle. "Oh, Meggie. Come fast."

Chapter Twenty-one

Ronnelle's hair was rolled up in a dozen rag curlers; a thick layer of cream almost covered her face. She reached out and hugged Lulu and me at the same time, twirling us around together, leaving a smear of the cream on my cheek. "Oh, Meggie," she said, "I've gotten the best news!"

We went back to sit in her living room and she picked up her husband Michael's letter. "It's dated days ago. On his way home by ship." She sounded breathless. "He'll take a train and meet me in Detroit."

"When?" I asked.

"I don't know." She shook her head, the curlers bouncing. "He didn't know." She leaned forward. "I'm just going.

This weekend I'll wait in the station, a day, two days at most. It'll be crowded with people coming and going. Safe. I'll just be glad to be there."

I pictured what it would be like for us to hear that Eddie was coming on a train to Detroit. Ronnelle knew what I was thinking. She took my hand, and then we both noticed that, on the floor, Lulu was pulling at my shoelaces, knotting them together, humming a song without words that sounded like the Uncle Don song on the radio.

"There's something I'd like you to do for me, Meggie," Ronnelle said. "We'll ask your mother to be sure it's all right. Will you take care of Lulu for me? I can't bring her to the station. It's just during the day until I come back. The babysitter will be here at night."

I was nodding. No school Saturday or Sunday. Why not? *Carpe diem.* I'd never babysat before.

"I trust you, Meggie. You have a head on your shoulders. I know you can do this."

What had Eddie said? *No more baby, Meggie.*

On Saturdays Mom had to go to work, but she came over to kiss Ronnelle goodbye, and we both watched as Ronnelle drew a careful pencil line up the back of her leg. "To look like seams," she said. "I ran my last pair of silk stockings." She shrugged. "No more silk until after the war, but at least I can look as if I'm wearing them."

Mom gave her a last hug and told her to be careful. I sat on the floor playing with Lulu, watching Ronnelle comb her hair into a pageboy. She looked beautiful with her eyes sparkling. I even liked her freckles.

A little later, Dad and I went to the bus stop with her. Lulu clung to my shoulder, calling *"Bye-bye."* Ronnelle leaned out the bus window, wearing Pan-Cake makeup and bright red lipstick. "I love you," she called. "We'll be back soon. Both of us."

We walked home, Dad saying, "I miss the sound of the Sundae, Monday, and Always ice cream truck. Maybe Arnold has gone into the army at last."

I nodded. I knew that Arnold's bag was packed. He was leaving any day now, probably to finish the war in the Pacific, but I'd never say anything about the medal. That part was a secret. No one knew about it but Grandpa and me.

I waited until Dad had gone to bed and Lulu had fallen asleep on her blanket in the living room. Then I went into the hall closet for clean sheets. I made my bed with them and dusted and mopped; then I tiptoed back into the living room to make up the foldout couch. That was where I'd be sleeping from now on.

Patches and I were going to plaster up the hole in the wall. She said she knew how to do it, and that we could talk just as easily on the way to school every morning. Patches, who had blisters on both heels, who said it wasn't so terrible not to have shoes after all. Patches, who had become a friend I'd have forever, even after the war was over. We had promised each other that when we were grown, she'd find Rockaway and I'd find the mountains of Tennessee. And in the meantime, we could always write.

I looked around. Everything was ready. There was nothing I could do about Eddie except hope.

But there was something I'd been able to do about Grandpa.

Chapter Twenty-two

On Sunday we went to Mass together, Dad and Mom, Lulu and me. Lulu stretched herself out on the pew and lay there quietly through the whole service, taking her thumb out of her mouth only once. She pointed up at a stained-glass window of a man in a garden. A bird was perched on one of his hands.

"Who?" she asked.

"St. Francis, I think," I whispered back, looking at the stained-glass lilies around him. He could almost have been Grandpa in his garden in Rockaway. But I knew Grandpa wouldn't be in his garden today.

After church we stopped at the bakery for Danish pastries with cheese in the center like golden suns, and ate them walking home. And as we turned the corner, we saw Ronnelle and her husband, Michael, tall and very skinny, standing at our front door.

I let go of Lulu's hand so she could run to them, but she didn't. She stood there, her mouth covered with crumbs, just staring at them.

Michael came down the walk slowly with Ronnelle in back of him, and there were tears in his eyes. He knelt down in front of Lulu and said, "I've been waiting to see you forever."

"Are you Daddy?" she asked.

Ronnelle's outstretched hands were clasped, the veil on her blue hat a little crooked, and she was crying, too.

And then Michael was hugging Lulu, not minding her sticky face, and Mom nudged Dad and me. "Let them have some time," and we went into the house.

The morning went on and on. I wanted to say a million things to Mom, silly things like *Why don't you put a pot of coffee on?* or *Guess it'll seem strange that I'll be sleeping on the couch.*

I closed my teeth tight so I didn't say any of it, but I spent the morning, heart thudding, going from the window to the door, and at last it was noon, and I couldn't bear it anymore. "How about . . . ," I said to Mom as she sliced tomatoes for sandwiches. She looked at me over her shoulder. ". . . putting on a little lipstick," I finished.

Noon, he had written. *By noon at the latest*, and he was never late. But the church bells had rung, it was after noon, and I thought about his old car. *"You don't have to worry about me,"* he had said when we said goodbye. But I was going to tell him I *did* have to worry about him, I was glad to worry about him.

Next door I could hear Michael laughing. "Nice," I told Mom, "for Lulu to have her father." I smiled to myself, watching her.

She layered the tomato on the bread and cut a cucumber to put on top. She began to say something, but she never finished. The knife clattered into the sink as she looked out the window.

A car was pulling up in front, sounding loud, sounding terrible. But it had made it, just like our old Ford.

Mom ran her hands down her apron, and then we were out the door together, yelling back to Dad, "Wake up! Hurry!"

Grandpa tipped that terrible hat to us, then put his arms out, and we flew into them. "Margaret," he said, looking down at me.

"Yes," I told him as soon as I could talk. "Welcome home."

> *Dear Eddie,*
>
> *I'm putting this letter away for you. We'll open both envelopes when you come home.*
>
> *There are so many things I want to tell you, and I don't want to forget any of them.*
>
> *First, outside the door we have a salad garden growing.*

I planted it late, but a few of the seeds finally came up. The lettuce never turned into heads, but I'm going to cut the leaves tonight and they'll taste fine. We even have one cucumber started; it's no bigger than my thumb, but still, it will make a fine pickle.

That's what Grandpa said.

Grandpa is here now. I wrote to him and sent my five dollars from winning the contest so he could take the bus.

But that's not what he did. He said he had enough gas for his car to get here, and that we'd save the five dollars for when we see the sights in New York.

That first night Grandpa and I sat on the steps. I told him that my friend Arnold's garden needed taking care of, and he said, "That's a job for us." He said we have to do things for each other. He thinks that's the only way the wars might stop.

Dear Eddie. We sit at the table having dinner every night, looking at your picture.

I know you're coming, too. I'm waiting for you. We all are. I have hope.

Love,

Margaret

About the Author

Patricia Reilly Giff is the author of many beloved books for children, including the Kids of the Polk Street School books, the Friends and Amigos books, and the Polka Dot Private Eye books. Several of her novels for older readers have been chosen as ALA Notable books and ALA Best Books for Young Adults. They include *The Gift of the Pirate Queen*; *All the Way Home*; *Nory Ryan's Song*, a Society of Children's Book Writers and Illustrators Golden Kite Honor Book for Fiction; and the Newbery Honor Books *Lily's Crossing* and *Pictures of Hollis Woods*. *Lily's Crossing* was also chosen as a *Boston Globe–Horn Book* Honor Book.

Patricia Reilly Giff lives in Connecticut.